Drone Journalism:
Bird's eye view of storytelling

Drone Journalism:
Bird's eye view of storytelling

Bharat
Dr. Abid Ali

Dedication

"This book is dedicated to My Daughter, Yashasvi - the sweetest little sunshine ever"

Contents

Preface

Drone Journalism: Bird's eye view of storytelling investigates the dilemmas and opportunity of using drones for mass communication and journalistic purposes in a global perspective. The book explores drone journalism from multiple perspectives, including introduction to drone journalism, drones in India, drone journalism and regulatory challenge in India, drones transforming broadcast and media industry, drone journalism scenario in world, drone journalism: a story telling medium and 10 techniques to become a successful drone journalist. By widening the discussion of drone journalism, the book is ideal for mass communication and journalism students, teachers and research scholars, as well as drone developers and citizens with an interest in the responsible use of camera drones.

Chapter-1

Introduction to Drone Journalism

Introduction to Drones:

Drones are also known as –unmanned aerial systems (UAS)‖ or –remotely piloted aircraft systems (RPAS)‖. A drone is a flying vehicle that is programmed or remotely piloted to perform autonomous actions. In journalism industry, drones are often referred to as flying robots or camera drones. More commonly, they are known as unmanned aerial vehicles (UAVs), unmanned aerial systems (UASs) or remotely piloted aircrafts (RPAs). The news events such as sports events, warfare, protests, floods, fires, and underwater operations exemplify only a snippet of what might possibly be covered in outstanding ways with unmanned aerial vehicles available to reporters.

Photo: Craig Wilkinson

100

Introduction to Drone Journalism:

Drone journalism is the capture of video and still images by remotely operated or autonomous drones (more formally known as unmanned aerial vehicles or UAV) to record events for report by news agencies and citizen media. Drone journalism is often used to get stories that might go unreported due to risk of personal injury to reporters. Drone journalism, like drone photography in general, enables the gathering of information about events and persons of interest from a distance or altitude. In that way, it can often survey subjects that could not otherwise be monitored because of heights, angles and other environmental factors. Drones small size, their ability to fly and their ability to tolerate harsh environments mean that they can survey subjects and events in places that people cannot easily go, such as a volcano or a war zone.

Photo: Ayomide Ayano

The Drones offer interesting perspectives for journalism and media industry. Drones equipped with cameras can take photos and videos from an aerial perspective, reaching inaccessible places or offering breathtaking footage. Still, journalists might hesitate to use drones for their work, because there are too many issues and unclear regulations. Drones equipped with cameras can take photos and videos from an aerial perspective that can be integrated into everyday news coverage. Reporters can either directly integrate the material into their online or TV news outlets, or they can indirectly make use of the materials as a source to feed their stories (especially in ethically critical cases).

Definition of Drone journalism:

Drone Journalism refers to the utilization of drones as newsgathering mean in a wide range of journalism and mass communication services. A simpler and stricter definition has been provided by Matt Waite, who runs the Drone Journalism Lab: –It's using a small unmanned aircraft to gather photo, video, and data for journalism‖ (Whitaker, 2016). While the definitions describe the typical uses of drones in journalism, there are also some not such obvious cases. Hence, UAVs can collect additional data offered by the embedded sensors (i.e. invisible /infrared light cameras, atmospheric pollution measures, smoke detection, location and geographical information, and others), so they can be utilized in Data Journalism and associated news /story validation processes.

Drone journalism is an innovative and exciting way to tell stories. But this technology also brings understandable safety and privacy concerns. Drones are becoming increasingly widespread in journalism sector. This should not come as a surprise: as drone and camera tech matures, it becomes not only better but also more affordable. Modern drones can fly higher, faster, are easier to handle, and can carry high-resolution cameras. In the hands of a skilled operator, drones are capable of generating breathtaking footage that would otherwise be far beyond the realm of possibility. So, if you purchased a shiny new drone and are eager to put your new toy to use, Johnny Miller, a Code for Africa news fellow specializing in drone photography and journalism, shares his top insights to utilizing drones to their full potential.

Drones and Journalism explores the increased use of unmanned aerial vehicles, or drones, by the global media for researching and newsgathering purposes. Phil Chamberlain examines the technological development and capabilities of contemporary drone hardware and the future of drone journalism. He also considers the complex place of the media's drone use in relation to international laws, as well as the ethical challenges and issues raised by the practice. Drones can be used to do many things. In this instance, this remote controlled helicopter in Berlin is supposed to apply artificial DNA to cables of a telecommunications company in order to prevent thefts of copper.

In the present scenario, the drones, or unmanned aircraft systems (UAS) are used in every field of journalism including photography, videography, film making, wedding photography, media research and many more. According to the Federal Aviation Administration, "an unmanned aircraft is a device that is used, or is intended to be used, for flight in the air with no onboard pilot". The use of drones for information collection in the journalism industry is still new.

The concept of drone journalism was first explored in 2002 at The Poynter Institute for Media Studies by Larry Larsen who looked at the ethical and practical use of unmanned aerial vehicles for reporting and media research. Larsen taught journalists from around the world about the capabilities and possibilities of using an unmanned aerial vehicle for investigative reporting and in the summer of 2003 built the first UAV specifically for drone journalism using a quadcopter platform streaming wireless video that was recorded in the field using an Archos AV300.

In 2012 Matt Waite founded the University of Nebraska-Lincoln's Drone Journalism Lab to explore how drones can be used for reporting. More specifically, the lab's purpose is to provide a place for the study of the ethicality, legality, and practicality of drone use in journalism. The lab's website plays a key role in the drone journalism debate, as it provides an online discussion platform, as well as links to and analysis of research and news articles. In 2013 Waite received a cease-and-desist notice from the Federal Aviation Administration.

According to Miller, in order to be a good drone journalist, you must be prepared to use your drone sparingly and only when necessary."There is not a good set of precedents for how drones and drone footage can be legally used, which means operating them sometimes falls into a grey area. Use your intuition. Think of how you would react if you were witnessing someone else flying the drone in the same way," he wrote.

Drones can be programmed to capture multiple high-resolution photographs from different angles and shots, which can be combined to create photorealistic 3D models through the principles of photogrammetric. These graphical models can be then exploited in immersive stories and virtual /augmented reality services (VR/AR) that are considered as the next big thing in Journalism. Apparently, these innovative services trigger active audience collaboration and enhancement and they have been used for raising public awareness in various circumstance. Characteristic examples are the (civil war) Syria Project (http://www.immersivejournalism.com/project-syria-premieres-at-the-world-economicforum/), the Dandora Dumpsite in Nairobi, Kenya (https://ejatlas.org/conflict/dandoralandfill-in-nairobi-kenya), and others (Corcoran, 2015; Ogleby & Joshi 2016; Tremayne & Clark 2014; Whitaker 2016)

Among the most popular Drone Journalism use case scenarios it can be listed the nuclear disaster of Fukushima Daiichi, Japan, in March 2011. For evident reasons, the hazardous environment could not be directly accessed from ground or air, the same time that questions were arisen regarding the validity of the radiation level measurements, which were taken and announced by the Japanese government. Hence, news organizations had no other choice in validating the given data but to compare them with those of other official agencies, reporting important deviations when observed.

A year later, drone technology was applied in the Fukushima, gathering images and associated information, thus providing a much more sophisticated and accurate solution to the above reporting problem. Likewise, drone journalism could be the ideal tool for reporting physical disasters (e.g. an earthquake or hurricane, etc.), while offering valuable civil protection informing services to the public (Culver 2014). We are not far from the moment that drones would become a common news reporting tool and/or an indispensable item of most media organization or freelancer's backpack (Corcoran 2015). Drones are very useful on newsgathering, where immediate and geographically unconstrained coverage is valuable (i.e. major conflicts, civil unrests, disaster coverage and relief: floods, fires, earthquakes, etc.).

Additional cases include environmental journalism, aerial surveillance, nature monitoring, wildlife protection, sports coverage and retrieval, investigation and documentation of crimes and generally illegal activities, where, besides immediacy and mobility, multiple viewpoints are essential. Drones are very important in hostile and hazardous environments, where human approach is considered dangerous and unsafe, and/or when ground coverage is not feasible; there is also the ‒disposable drone scenario‖, where it is expected that UAVs might not return to the land zone (Corcoran 2015; Ogleby & Joshi 2016). Featured documentaries have also been created using drone footage, like the ‒Auschwitz: Drone video of Nazi concentration camp‖ (https://youtu.be/449ZOWbUkf0) and the ‒Postcards from Pripyat, Chernobyl‖ (https://vimeo.com/112681885).

Journalists throughout the world are increasingly using Remote Piloted Aerial System, aka Drones, to capture news events. RPAS are particularly valuable for journalists covering natural disasters, in that they can video the crumbling devastation for the global audience, while the journalist stays on safer terrain. The safety issue for disaster field reporters is becoming more pressing, as scientists predict bigger and more frequent devastating weather episodes, therefore more reliance on Drone Journalism to safely capture the visuals for news outlets.

According to Bellows (2013), drones ‒stand poised to revolutionize the media in much the same way the Internet has changed the print media‖ (p. 596). This is partially because many drones are inexpensive and fairly easy to operate. Small drones can maneuver into spaces where manned aircraft could not. They might also minimize danger in hazardous situations where a pilot's life might be at risk. But there are some potential downsides of drone use in journalism. As Tremayne and Clark (2014) pointed out, ‒The implications for the field of journalism and mass communication are numerous, with practical, theoretical and ethical dimensions‖ (p. 232).

Roug (2014) has asserted that some drone video has had ‒a vivid, eyewitness feel that far surpassed the quality of shots from cameramen behind yellow police tape‖ (p. 29). She equates the potential transformative effect of drones in journalism with other technology, claiming that it is ‒on par with the advent of cell phone cameras and Twitter‖ (p. 30). Schoyer (2013) added that drones could allow journalists to gather information and images currently available only from the government. He pointed out that many stations used aerial shots of the aftermath following tropical storm Sandy—which is great, except that –all those pictures came from the government‖ (paragraph 15). If journalists rely on the government for video, it puts all of the power into the hands of the institution journalists should be striving to keep in check.

Drones have many potential uses in journalism, ranging from disaster coverage to protests, traffic reports, and even sporting events. In fact, they have already been used internationally for all of these purposes (Berry, 2014; Culver, 2014; Tremayne & Clark, 2014; Waite, 2014; Winslow, 2012). Tremayne and Clark (2014) have suggested that putting aerial surveillance technology in the hands of the people, especially journalists, –_reverses the panoptic gaze' then the watched become the watchers‖ (p. 233).

This gives power to the citizens to _police' the police—bringing to light issues such as racial profiling or abuse of power. This is an extension of the power already gained through the use of mobile devices and social media. Ubayasiri (2009) has suggested that the use of satellite and drone video in Sri Lanka made it possible for the world to open a dialog about the alleged abuses, which might have been otherwise censored by the government. Without that video, –the much needed debate on the human suffering and the civilian death toll may have been non-existent‖ (p. 1). Similar _watchdog' drone videos have shown protests around the world (Bellows, 2013; Tremayne & C

Video is only one of many potential uses for drones in journalism. Drones might be used to carry a multitude of data-gathering devices, including geographic information systems to map the extent of wildfires, or sensors to measure radiation levels, wind speeds, or thermal images (Bellows, 2013; Culver, 2014; Schroyer, 2013). The ability to gather this type of data opens up the possibility of an entirely –new form of reporting, offering to the UAS operator a completely new way to discover, investigate, and track a story‖ (Bellows, 2013, p. 612).

Chapter-2

Drones in India

The Age of Drones:

All you need to know about India's attempts to produce unmanned aerial vehicles the world's military forces are going unmanned – some quickly, others gradually. And India is no exception. After a rather desultory phase lasting two decades, when the high cost of imported systems kept their numbers low, the future is beginning to look distinctly brighter for the nation's armed forces. The government's _Make in India' initiative, despite skepticism from some quarters, is encouraging private firms to take interest in manufacturing unmanned surveillance devices and weapon systems for use by the Indian Army, the Indian Navy and the Indian Air Force (IAF).

This also offers an excellent opportunity to break the stranglehold of the state-owned Defense Research and Development Organization (DRDO) over all research and development activities into unmanned aerial systems in the country. And it comes not a day too soon, because not only are India's potential adversaries rapidly building up their unmanned capability, but a variety of non-state actors are likely to follow suit. For decades the United States (US) held the edge in the development and use of unmanned systems, especially of the airborne variety, with Israel close behind. Few other countries had access to the technology and even fewer actually used such systems to carry out strikes or attacks. But now more military forces are venturing down the unmanned route, convinced of the manifest advantages of such systems.

**Flying drones in India will be legal from December 1 2018
(Getty file photo)**

Unmanned aerial vehicles (UAV) or ‑drones‖ as they are loosely called were originally used purely for reconnaissance. They are now routinely employed for communications, electronic warfare (EW) and a plethora of other roles. Indeed the variety and number of a nation's inventory of UAVs and their fiery cousins, unmanned combat air vehicles (UCAV), is already a key predictor of its military might. Although the so-called ‑armed drone attacks‖ especially against terrorist leaders in the Middle East, Afghanistan and Pakistan attract global attention, the US is by no means alone in developing and deploying UCAVs and other unmanned systems. Russia is making good progress while keeping a low profile. China, which of late seems anxious to publicise its military prowess, claims growing capability across the spectrum of unmanned systems. It is beginning to threaten US dominance in some aspects.

Proliferation Problems - China has few inhibitions about sharing its weapons with countries such as Pakistan, Iraq, Nigeria, Saudi Arabia, Egypt and the United Arab Emirates. Pakistan is quite likely to be a recipient of the CH-5 export variant, not too long from now. Indeed, Pakistan already boasts of an indigenous armed UAV. In September 2015, the country's military forces fired a laser-guided air-to-surface missile named _Barq' from the Burraq drone. It was the first time the Burraq was used in a live military operation. Analysts believe it was developed with Chinese assistance and is closely related to China's own CH-3 UAV. China is destined to grow as a global exporter of UAVs and UCAVs and decades of US attempts to curb the spread of armed systems seem set to fail.

Tapas Triumphs - When it comes to the development of advanced weapon systems, India has so many things going for it – a strong industrial base, vast human resources and the determination of many of its firms to constantly innovate. However, till now, unmanned military systems have been under the exclusive purview of DRDO, which DRDO has managed to make steady if unspectacular progress. Its latest milestone was the first flight of the Rustom-2 prototype on 16 November 2016. The Rustom-2 (redesignated Tapas 201) medium altitude long endurance (MALE) UAV took off from the Chitradurga aeronautical test range (ATR) in Karnataka and landed after 10 minutes. The mission achieved the modest objective of proving the flying characteristics of the platform, including take-off, level flight, ability to carry out turns and landing. Intensive flight testing to validate the design parameters is scheduled to continue for a period that may extend to a year or more. The DRDO plans to produce 10 such UAVs for test flights and follow an accelerated testing schedule so as to achieve flight certification in the shortest possible time. User validation trials will follow certification. The Tapas 201 has a length of 9.5m, wingspan of more than 20m and an empty weight of 1,800kg.

Its maximum speed is just 225 kmph, but it has an impressive endurance of more than 24 hours and it can operate up to an altitude of 35,000 feet above mean sea level. Based on the earlier Rustom-H variant, its lightweight airframe features an enhanced aerodynamic configuration, digital flight control and advanced navigation system. Tapas 201 takes off and lands from a runway which makes it safer to operate than older DRDO models. Its fuselage was built by Taneja Aerospace and Aviation Limited (TAAL), a private aerospace firm that specialises in manufacture of aircraft structural assemblies. The all-weather UAV is designed to carry a range of advanced equipment including electro-magnetic intelligence (ELINT), communication intelligence (COMINT), synthetic aperture radar (SAR), maritime patrol radar (MPR), radio altimeter, transmitting and receiving antennae and situational awareness payloads of up to 350kg.

It can fly either autonomously with an onboard flight control system that uses waypoint navigation or in manual mode controlled by an operator on the ground. The Tapas 201 is optimised for intelligence, surveillance and reconnaissance (ISR) tasks. It currently has no armed capability. The Indian armed forces are expected to order a total of around 80 of these UAVs to begin with. The naval variant will have specialised maritime surveillance sensors. A Brief History of DRDO's Unmanned Endeavour - Before Rustom-2, there was Rustom-1 MALE UAV that first flew in October 2010 and since then has undergone much testing. It is an all-weather system designed to operate at medium to long ranges and gather near real time, high quality imagery and signals.

It was the first indigenous UAV with conventional take-off and landing capability. Although it has been undergoing trials to integrate the indigenous HELINA anti-tank missile, these efforts have failed to bear fruit. The Indian Army wants DRDO to speedily complete the Rustom-1 project and will place orders only if its performance is found satisfactory. Nishant - The Nishant UAV that entered service hazardous objects safely. Capable of being remotely controlled over a range of 500m line-of-sight (LOS) or even within buildings, it is an important asset in the hands of the Indian Army, Police and Paramilitary Forces. The Indian Navy too needs unmanned craft.

Apart from surface vessels, unmanned underwater vehicles (UUV) are invaluable for mine counter-measure (MCM) operations, naval ISR roles and anti-submarine warfare (ASW) missions. There are two broad types of UUVs: autonomous undersea vehicles (AUVs) that can operate independently without human inputs for most or all phases of operation and remotely operate dundersea vehicles (ROVs) where a human operator is essential. UUVs have the potential to revolutionize naval warfare just as UAVs are transforming air-land warfare. The Naval Science and Technological Laboratory (NSTL), Visakhapatnam, under the DRDO, is developing various AUVs small and large. It is currently working on an AUV that is four metres long, 1.4m wide, weighs 1,500kg and can take a 500kg payload. It has a speed of about seven kmph and a depth rating of 400m. According to NSTL, with the completion of user evaluation trials, the AUV's basic design is ready.

Work on the customised design will commence once the Indian Navy finalises its qualitative requirements (QRs). The Indian Navy is expected to order 10 such AUVs for ISR, mine mitigation and sensor deployment, communication couriers and for target practice during exercises. The Inevitability of Imports - As with most weapon systems of the three services, the process of induction of UAVs began with imports. The Indian Army was first off the blocks in 1996, when it began operating the Searcher Mk I tactical surveillance UAV acquired from Israel Aerospace Industries (IAI). The IAF and the Indian Navy quickly followed suit. By 2000, the Searcher Mk II entered service and a year later the Heron 1 MALE UAV. Both these systems are also manufactured by IAI. The pace of induction has been very slow. Between them, the three services have only about 100 Searcher Mk IIs, while 50 to 60 Heron 1s are shared between the IAF and the Indian Navy. However, for the last year or two, the outlook has been rapidly improving, because of increased government commitment as well as its June 2016 decision to join the Missile Technology Control Regime (MTCR).

Some estimates are that India is likely to procure more than 5,000 UAVs over the next 10 years at a cost of over $3 billion. These include high altitude long endurance (HALE) UAVs, MALE UAVs, vertical take-off and landing (VTOL) UAVs and tactical UAVs going all the way down to mini- and micro-UAVs for the Indian Army. The Army proposes to provision UAVs even at the battalion level. In November 2016, the high-powered Defence Acquisition Council (DAC) approved the purchase of 598 mini-UAVs for the infantry, under the _Buy Indian' category. According to official sources, they will be used for aerial surveillance of areas up to five to seven kilometres ahead of the area of responsibility.

The IAF and the Indian Navy will also have several squadrons each of surveillance UAVs and UCAVs.

It is estimated that the Indian armed forces plan to induct over 200 armament-capable UAVs in the next 10 years. In November 2016, the Indian government signed a $400-million deal to purchase 10 IAI Heron TP UAVs (also known as Eitan) for the IAF. Delivery is expected to commence within two to three years. This will give the country its first known capability to launch guided weapons and lightweight air-to-ground tactical missiles from an unmanned platform. It will be an invaluable asset should more cross-border surgical strikes be planned.

The Heron TP has a wingspan of 26m and length of 14m. According to the manufacturer, it has a maximum take-off weight of 4,650kg and carries a typical mission payload of 1,000kg. It is powered by a 1,200 HP turboprop engine and has an impressive endurance of 36 hours. Its range is beyond line of sight (BLOS) with SATCOM (satelite communications) Major Imports From The US - Of even greater importance is the possibility that India will purchase advanced UAVs and UCAVs from the US. Most likely to be inducted are 22 Predator XP unarmed UAVs for the Indian Navy.

The IAF is looking to purchase 100 General Atomics Predator C Avenger next generation, multi-mission UCAVs. This would make India the largest operator of this UCAV in the world. The jet powered Avenger has a length of 13m and wingspan of 20m. Its maximum take-off weight is 8,255kg. Its internal and total payload capacity is 1,588kg and 2,948kg respectively. It has several stealth features including reduced radar and heat signature as well as internal weapons storage. Are all these proposed acquisitions part of a plan? They are Since getting enough combat aircraft is proving such a daunting task and may take perhaps a couple of decades, military planners are trying to quickly increase the IAF's firepower through armed UAVs and UCAVs.

These may also be more suitable than manned combat jets for the no-war no-peace situation that prevails along India's western border. They would be the system of choice to take out terrorist camps or infrastructure and might lead the first wave against enemy air defence systems or vital targets deep inside enemy territory in the event of an all-out war. A Brighter Unmanned

Future Depends On the Private Sector - Of late, the Indian government has renewed its efforts to make up for lost time and manufacture or import various types of unmanned systems in large numbers, realising that they will be an important factor in any future conflict. There is a crying need for the DRDO to be more realistic in its claims of successes and rosy projections for the future, as well as more reliable in its development time and cost estimate. Critical technologies necessary for UAV operation cannot be developed overnight. For instance, key to safe aerial unmanned operations outside of military airspace is a compact and foolproof collision avoidance system and this is still not available indigenously.

The Tapas 201 (Rustom-2) is the first really capable UAV to emerge from DRDO's stable. Its speedy readiness and smooth induction in the Indian military could mark a turning point in DRDO's performance. But key to the process will be the organisations ability to stick to deadlines and cost estimates as well as to deliver a product of impeccable quality. Further in the future is DRDO's autonomous unmanned research aircraft (AURA) for the IAF and the Indian Navy. The design work is to be carried out by the Aeronautical Development Agency (ADA). AURA is planned as a stealthy UCAV, capable of internal and external weapon carriage. Currently, almost the entire inventory of the nation's operational UAVs is imported.

There is a growing realisation that unless the private sector is involved in a big way, it will be impossible to even partially satisfy the demand for military unmanned systems through indigenous sources. To encourage a future that will be less dependent on the DRDO, many major UAV systems can be outsourced to competent and qualified Indian firms. It is heartening that various systems of the Tapas 201 such as the airframe, landing gear and sub-systems for flight control and avionics, were developed within the country with the collaboration of private industries. According to Tata Advanced Systems Limited (TASL), the firm is well-positioned to build entire aircraft and UAVs for defence customers under the _Make in India' programme.

Reliance Defence and L&T Heavy Engineering too are quite capable of developing and manufacturing small UAVs on their own and they can gradually move up the value chain. Therefore, even for imports, tenders are to be restricted to domestic companies that can tie up with foreign firms to _Make in India'. India's holdings of unmanned systems are clearly inadequate for a country of this size. This is, perhaps, due to uncertain commitment from the users in the past, inadequate funding and over-reliance on the DRDO's ability to deliver.

Consequently, precious time has been lost. Pakistan is well on the way to acquiring a respectable unmanned military capability with assured help from China. China itself has forged so far ahead that India has no realistic hope of matching its capability in the foreseeable future. Concerted efforts are, therefore, necessary to equip the country's armed forces with adequate UAVs and other unmanned systems for critical ISR tasks as well as to meet the threat of cross-border terrorist attacks. It will help them better address the complex security challenges the country faces.

What You Need to Know About Drones in India

Mumbai became the first city to have a margarita pizza delivered via drone. Flying over the traditional lunch delivery system the army of dabbawalas who shuttle lunchboxes to offices all over the city the pizza-drone, which was launched from Francesco's Pizzeria, made sense in a city known for its history of atypical and innovative delivery solutions. Under current regulations, the use of drones for commercial purposes is still illegal in India. Francesco's Pizzeria sidestepped the law by delivering the pie to the owner's _friend'—not a _customer'—and thus technically did not engage in a commercial transaction. Perhaps inspired by the delivery of the margarita pizza, e-retail behemoth Amazon plans to use Mumbai and Bangalore as the trial launch pad for their Prime Air delivery system. Drones are becoming serious business in India, both in the commercial and military spheres. As the country becomes a big player in the drone game, here's what you need to know:

India first used military drones during the 1999 Kargil War with Pakistan. Army search and reconnaissance missions proved to be incredibly difficult, if not nearly impossible, without air support. The Indian Air Force deployed manned English Canberra PR57 aircraft for photo reconnaissance along the Line of

Control, but this system proved highly inefficient and strategically weak over the mountainous Kargil terrain.

After India lost a Canberra PR57 to Pakistani infrared homing missiles, Israel discreetly supplied the Indian Air Force with IAI Heron and Searcher drones, which were useful for acquiring target information along the Line of Control. Since Kargil, India has procured a number of Israeli military unmanned aircraft. India's current arsenal includes the Israel Aerospace Industries Harpy and Harop unmanned combat aerial vehicles, and IAI Searcher and Heron unmanned aerial vehicles. In 2009, the Indian Air Force purchased 10 Harops in a $100 million contract with Israel Aerospace Industries. In February 2013, the Indian Air Force made a $280 million deal with Israel Aerospace Industries for a new series of Heron medium-altitude, long-endurance drones.

In late 2013, India's Ministry of Defense rejected an offer by Israel Aerospace Industries and India's Defense Research and Development Organization (DRDO) to jointly develop a new version of the Heron UAV. According to Israeli officials, India turned down the offer because of an internal struggle among Indian Defense officials, many of whom, they said, would rather stimulate India's domestic drone program than team up with Israel Aerospace Industries (this could not be confirmed). Israeli sources estimated the potential value of the project at several hundred million dollars.

In June of 2013, India began deploying Heron surveillance drones in a limited capacity over Maoist rebel strongholds in the east. Such activity has been limited to Andhra Pradesh-Odisha and Andhra-Chhattisgarh. These states are densely forested, however, so the UAVs have been of little use in reconnaissance and surveillance. India's Central Reserve Police Force claimed that an ambush last Monday that killed 14 of its soldiers could have been prevented if there had been a Heron UAV overhead.

Two weeks ago, a Heron UAV, used by the Indian Air Force for surveillance purposes crashed near the town of Bhuj in Gujrat. The downed UAV was reportedly spotted by startled villagers, who later reported the aircraft to the town's police commission. Indian Air Force officials are still unsure as to the cause of the crash, and a court of inquiry has been ordered.

India's Defense Research and Development Organization have also developed its own domestic UAV program. The project aims to develop a domestic arsenal to replace and augment the existing fleet of IAI vehicles. Here is a list of completed and pending DRDO projects:

1. **DRDO Lakshya**: a target drone used for discreet aerial reconnaissance and target acquisition. It is launched by solid propellant rocket motor and sustained by a turbojet engine in flight.

2. **DRDO Nishant**: primarily designed for intelligence-gathering over enemy territory and also for reconnaissance, training, surveillance, target designation, artillery fire correction, and damage assessment. The Nishant has completed its developmental phase and user trials.

3. **DRDO Aura**: similar to the Lockheed Martin RQ-170 Sentinel, a stealth drone that will be capable of releasing missiles, bombs, and precision-guided munitions. The details of the Aura project are still, for the most part, classified. Aura projected test date is set to be sometime in 2016.

4. **DRDO Rustom**: Modeled after the American Predator UAV, the Rustom is a Medium-Altitude Long-Endurance (MALE) system. Like the Predator, the Rustom is designed to be used for both reconnaissance and combat missions. The Rustom is still in prototype stage and is expected to replace and supplement Israeli Heron model UAVs in the Indian Air Force.

The Economic Times reported that Amazon Prime Air deliveries would be made in the cities of Bangalore and Mumbai before the Hindu festival of Diwali; the festival occurred in October, but no customer deliveries have been made to date.

Following Amazon's announcement, this past October the Directorate General of Civil Aviation announced that until proper rules and regulations are formulated, the use of drones by civilians will be illegal. The DGCA made an announcement on October 7th 2014: ―Till such regulations are issued, no non government agency, organization, or an individual will launch a UAS in Indian Civil Airspace for any purpose whatsoever.‖ No date has been given for these regulations. (This announcement likely explains Amazon's failure to begin testing Prime Air.)

In spite of the uncertain regulatory future, domestic startups are producing and using drones for both security and commercial purposes. Drones have been used to provide services ranging from disaster relief, security and surveillance, and aerial photography.

Here is a list of notable Indian drone startup companies:

1. **Social Drones**: A startup that ─designs and manufactures user friendly, easy to use, high-performance drones for social and unconventional applications.‖ Social Drones made news when its drones were used to provide disaster relief in Uttarakhand after severe flooding in 2013. The company's drones were used to airdrop first aid kits to areas where relief efforts had been stalled, as well as to areas that were deemed unsafe for conventional relief methods.

2. **Airpix**: specializes in aerial photography and video production. Clients include real estate agents, tourism organizations, to journalists in disaster zones. After floods ravaged the Indian state of Uttarakhand in June of 2013, Airpix drone photography was used in a campaign to rebuild Uttarakhand to spread awareness about infrastructural deficiencies in the mountainous state.

3. **Garuda Robotics**: started by 20-year old college drop-out, Pulkit Jaiswal, Garuda produces software to gather and analyze data collected by drones. The company also produces software to control unmanned aircraft. Garuda markets its products for a variety of uses that range from land and agricultural surveys to security, search and rescue, and logistics.

4. **Edall Systems**: a Bangalore-based company that provides engineering, design and manufacturing services, drone development, and unmanned aerial vehicle training programs for students and professionals. The company also builds parts for India's National Aerospace Labs, as well as the Defense Research and Development Organization.

5. **Idea Forge**: recently developed the Netra UAV in collaboration with the DRDO. The Netra UAV is a surveillance quadcopter drone used primarily by India's Central Reserve Police Force and the Uttar Pradesh Special Task Force.

Although Idea Forge primarily focuses on security and surveillance services, it also provides a services such as geographical mapping and surveying, oil and gas pipeline monitoring, aerial cinematography, crowd management, real estate photography, and event management.

6. **Aurora Integrated Systems**: a Bangalore-based company that provides drone technology to India's Defense Research and Development Organization as well as directly to the Indian Army. The company's fleet includes the Urban View, a lightweight reconnaissance drone, and the Altius MK-II, a medium-range, medium-altitude autonomous vehicle that can be used for surveillance, target acquisition, and reconnaissance.

Draft guidelines issued by the Directorate General of Civil Aviation (DGCA)

It regulates the civil application of drones. It allows the taking of _pictures' but is silent on _drone reporting'. The DGCA, being an aviation regulatory authority in India, can regulate any matter directly or incidentally related to aviation activities. Policies on drone journalism must address matters like liability in the case of damage due to drone operation.

Vicarious liability in tort law is also in question, as the drone will be used by a reporter on behalf of his employer (a news organization), to whom a Unique Identification Number is to be issued under the Draft Guidelines. In such a situation, drones can only be deployed when alternative means are not suitable and when the user is properly trained. The _newsworthiness' of the information must be the paramount concern.

There are also other issues that must still be considered before using drones for journalistic purposes. Being an intrusive technology, drones are likely to have some privacy implications. Unfortunately, the DGCA guidelines clearly missed the privacy issue by mentioning only that ─due importance‖ must be given to privacy but failing to lay out any procedures. Privacy has been considered as a fundamental right under Article 21 of the Indian Constitution by the Supreme Court. This right is not absolute and the state can limit it if required by a public emergency or public safety, provided that the limitation is reasonable and established by law.

The use of drones naturally presents a great threat to data protection and privacy. The existing Information Technology Act 2000 and its amended version are insufficient to mitigate this threat, as they do not address violations of privacy in the case of aerial surveillance. Even the recently passed Aadhaar Act 2016, that allows collecting an individual's demographic and biometric information for targeted delivery of subsidies, benefits, and services, does not mention privacy.

A possible solution is to enact new legislation (either in the form of the Draft Bill on the Right to Privacy or another amendment to the Information Technology Act) to include drone surveillance. But this is cumbersome. A more plausible solution is for the DGCA to come up with policies protecting privacy, such as prohibiting news agencies from retaining pictures taken by drones unless required by law or for some investigation as a piece of evidence. It must be made a part of public policy that those pictures be accessible for public scrutiny unless exempted by law. The media has to follow the basic ethical norms laid out in the Norms of Journalistic Conduct 2010, which states that the media –shall not intrude or invade the privacy of an individual, unless outweighed by genuine overriding public interest, not being a prurient or morbid curiosity‖.

The best way for the DGCA to develop privacy regulations for drone surveillance is to adhere to the basic principle of –reasonableness:‖ the reasonableness of the drone surveillance and the reasonableness of the citizen's expectation of privacy should be balanced against each other. Airspace is of course common property but the reasonable expectation of privacy should limit its common use. Hence, in the absence of black-letter law, the DGCA must come up with a sustainable and comprehensive policy for drone journalism. Journalists and lawyers should be involved in this process of policy formulation.

*****

Chapter- 3

Drones Journalism and regulatory challenge in India

Drones are very powerful tools to provide high-resolution images and terrain information required for projects related to infrastructure development or natural resource management. In India, a country of 1.4 billion people and beset by various challenges relating to resource management and impacts of climate change, drones have the potential to make infrastructure climate-resilient, saving enormous sums of money and improving the lives and livelihoods of millions.

However, the scientific applications of drones in India have remained limited so far primarily due to (a) a fairly restrictive policy on usage of drones, (b) lack of adequate expertise to apply drone surveys for scientific applications, (c) safety and security concerns related to drone operations. It is widely believed that the benefits that can be accrued from the application of drones in various sectors significantly outweigh the problems and risks perceived by the concerned agencies and the wider public. Therefore, a critical understanding of the power of this technology and its applications is necessary. This technology has a long way to go, and a fast-growing economy like India's cannot afford to lag behind in applying this technology.

As a part of the Frontier Technology Live streaming (FTL) project supported by DFID, a pilot was taken up (see previous Medium Post on this) to identify and champion the use of drones for all Mahatma Gandhi National Rural Employment Guarantee Act (MGNREGA) projects of the Government of India. The MGNREGA is a very large program to support the construction of small infrastructure projects by providing at least 100 days of guaranteed wage employment in a financial year to every household whose adult members volunteer to do unskilled manual work.

The FTL pilot was designed to demonstrate that the planning, monitoring, and evaluation of the assets created through the MGNREGA projects can be significantly enhanced through the use of drones. As a part of this pilot, first an in-field design for using the drones on planning the MGNREGA projects was developed, and then surveys were undertaken for three representative sites across India for demonstrating the advantages and benefits from this technology.

1. A pilot in Chhattisgarh state was aimed at designing check dams and farm pond, the most common water harvesting structures in this region (see photo below);
2. A pilot in Odisha explored the ways to mitigate land degradation using drone technology;
3. A pilot in Bihar attempted to revive the age-old Ahaar-pine system of irrigation in rural areas using high-resolution images and topographic information generated through drones.

In addition to the MGNREGA projects, there are potential applications of drone mapping to enhance and support urban planning in India and to meet the specific needs and requirements that follows-on from the Smart City policy championed by the Ministry of Housing and Urban Affairs.

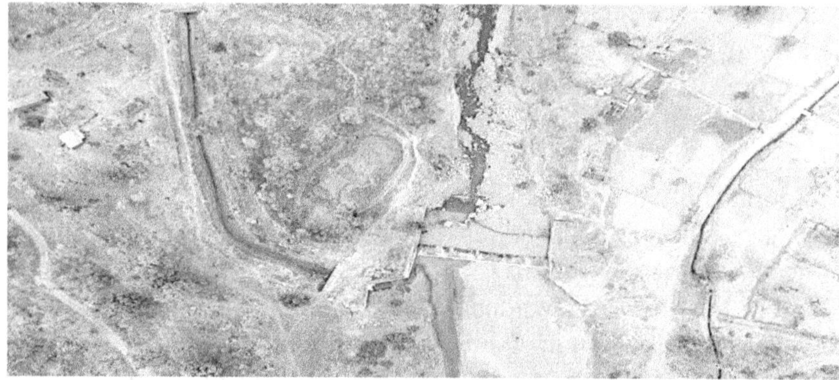

Photo 1: Drone image of a check dam in Chhattisgarh; High-resolution images like these and a synoptic view provides a very good perspective to plan and monitor these structures; these

images can also be used for generating high-resolution topographic information.

The Directorate General of Civil Aviation (DGCA) is the designated authority in India to regulate the use of drones in the country and they have released a set of drone-regulations on 27th August 2018. These regulations are targeted to formalize the productive use of drones for civilian applications both for scientific research and infrastructure planning in India in rural and urban sectors. This post highlights the major points of these regulations and provides suggestions to improve these regulations based on global best practices.

Classification of drones:

Before we proceed further, let us first understand the types of drones that are commercially available: Typically, drones are classified on the basis of its weight. The weight of a drone refers to the total weight of the drone and its payload and therefore determines its application to some extent. The DGCA regulations have proposed a weight-based classification of drones as (a) Nano (<250 gm), (b) Micro (>250 gm and < 2Kg), © Small (>2Kg but <25Kg), (d) medium (>25Kg but <150Kg) and (e) Large: (>150Kg).

For the purpose of rural and urban planning as well as for scientific research, the most applicable category is the Micro category. Therefore, most of the discussion in this chapter will be focused on micro drones.

Highlights of DGCA regulatory changes, and some concerns:

Regarding micro drones, a reading of the proposed DGCA regulations highlights several key points that all users should know before they start using the technology. This chapter also discusses the implications and concerns related to these regulations in terms of their applicability and viability.

All micro-drones will now require Unique Identification Number (UIN), insurance, fireproof ID, a radio frequency tags (RFID) and a SIM card allowing for tracking by the DGCA.

It is important to note that these requirements are not supported by current commercial technology and are also not obligatory in most western countries. In fact, there is no micro-drone in the current commercial market that can comply with these regulations! The development of these components would, therefore, require an investment of capital and this would dramatically increase the cost. Even if such technology becomes available as separate components, the affixing of these components to existing commercial drones presents increasing safety concerns as the addition of elements to an existing airframe can impact its aerodynamic performance. In simple terms, this will make all available drones in the commercial market unusable, and it is hard to understand why DGCA would want to do this unless there is a lack of understanding of its implications. This regulation, therefore, needs serious reconsideration.

In addition, the drones should have Equipment Type Approval (ETA) from the Wireless Planning and Coordination (WPC) Wing of Department of Telecommunications for operating in the de-licensed frequency band(s). In other words, all drones need to be approved to use radio frequencies!

Urban and rural planning agencies in India can derive great benefits from low-cost commercial drones, but it's too onerous for them to ask permission for radio frequency usage. Such permissions should only need to be obtained by the merchants who should be obliged to sell products that comply with Indian law on radio frequency usage. This will go a long way to popularize the use of drones for various applications.

Security clearance from Ministry of Home Affairs (MHA) would be required for (a) an individual citizen of India, and (b) an Indian company registered in India or elsewhere. The central and State Government institutions are not required to get MHA clearance.

While this is an important step from a security concern, it requires effective implementation in terms of ease of obtaining security clearances. At this stage, there is very little clarity on the steps to be followed and the process is yet to be made operational possibly due to technical difficulties.

Civilian drone operators will require an Unmanned aircraft Operator Permit (UAOP) equivalent to pilot's license, except for nano-drones operating below 15 m and micro-drone operating below 60m in uncontrolled airspace/enclosed premises.

Given the widespread use of micro drones, the exemption of micro drones from requiring UAOP would be useful. However, the limitation of 60m height is a little discouraging because most scientific operations fly at 100–120 meters.

Global practices of drone operations: an overview

It is important to view the DGCA regulations in a global context so that we understand their implications in terms of applicability and ease of implementation. It is crucial to make sure that the Indian regulations are at par with the best global practices so that we can compete globally for applying this technology for deriving socio-economic benefits.

A review of regulations for operating drones in different parts of the world suggests that there are several widely accepted practices:

1. Drones must be operated within line of sight of the pilot to ensure the safety of the instrument and to ensure connectivity with the base;
2. Flying heights for drones should be within 60 to 100 meters so as not to interfere with commercial flights;
3. Drones are restricted to fly over densely populated areas although there are no definite directions in terms of limits of urban areas.
4. Insurance is commonly required for operating drones so as to cover the public liability in case of any accidents etc.

Photo 3: Preparing a drone survey in an agriculture-dominated rural area

In the UK, for pilots who wish to fly drones commercially, a license is required and a _Permit for Commercial Operations' (PfCO) has to be obtained. This also gives the pilot some minor additional privileges e.g. (a) can operate drones within 50 meters of cities (urban, inhabited areas), (b) can use controlled airspace if granted permission by local Air Traffic Control and (c) Public liability insurance is required. In Germany, drones below 2 Kg require no licensing. Drones up to 25Kg may be flown, but above 2Kg licensing is required with the complexity of procedure proportional to the weight of the drone. However, public liability insurance is required. In France and Italy, flights over urban areas are permitted only by licensed pilots and they can be operated at altitudes up to 150m. Public liability insurance is also required.

It is also important to note that the drones, particularly those falling in micro category (<2 kg weight) do not appear to pose a direct threat to personal safety. The US Federal Aviation Agency (FAA) released a study in March 2017 which observed that drones falling on humans do NOT represent a critical danger except for minor injuries from spinning propeller blades that can be easily mitigated by blade guards.

Further, while some of these considerations are important for operating drones in urban areas, the considerations and operating contexts in other sectors, such as rural planning or mapping of natural resources such as forest cover and water resources, are different and therefore some context-specific regulations must be developed.

Key recommendations from Indian perspectives

Based on these considerations, we recommend that all stakeholders such as NITI AAYOG (National Institution for Transforming India), Ministries of Rural Development, Housing and Urban Affairs, Water Resources, Agriculture, Environment and Forests and several others engage with the DGCA and other concerned users in order to bring the following amendments to the current regulation proposals:

1. The **weight classification categories of drones** which determine the requirements for operators are too broad. For example, the lowest weight classification of 2–25 kilograms should be further segmented to allow those with the smallest drones of up to 7 or 10 kg to fly with fewer registration and safety requirements than those that would be required for drones between 7 kg and 25 kg in weight. This would allow for increased use of drones in agriculture and infrastructure planning while still maintaining strong safety controls for relatively larger and potentially more hazardous drones.

2. **A Risk-based regulation, as opposed to only weight based,** could be another potential option, as is followed by the European Aviation Safety Agency (EASA). This system is based on the level of perceived risk in drone operations and includes: (a) Open—low risk drone operations, which do require permissions, (b) Specific, for which risks need to be mitigated through operational limitations, equipment specifications and personnel involved, requires authorization, and (c)certified—similar to piloted aircraft in terms of risk involved; requires certification and licensing.

3. Maintain the need for a Unique ID number and tag, but move this process to a simple online application form. As per the proposed regulations, the approvals related to equipment type, operating frequency bands etc. also have to be obtained from the DGCA. Most of these technical requirements can be fulfilled by the manufacturer itself for DGCA clearance, meaning that these drones will effectively be –pre-certified.‖ This will expedite the entire process of clearance.

4. Also, it may be beneficial to exempt academic institutions and government organizations from the complex and lengthy process of obtaining permissions and clearances particularly if the use of drones involves developmental projects for societal benefits. At the very least, the process should be limited to providing details of the area of operation, intended applications and types of the drone to be flown etc.

5. Remove the need for micro-drones of less than 2KG to be equipped with RFID tags and SIM cards for tracking, as most of these already have the radio frequency tagging of drones. The DGCA may wish to engage with drone manufacturers to include such features in commercial products, but, at the present time, such requirements would cripple the rising drone industry and lead to India falling behind other nations such as China in the development of drone applications and in the associated economic benefits.

6. Eliminate the requirement for fireproof Identification tags. This regulation might be motivated by in-air accidents but seems to be an unworkable solution at this stage. The nano and mini drones are mass-produced consumer goods, not aviation standard designed systems and made from composite type material and therefore such certification would be difficult. There would also need to be the infrastructure required and the associated workload and costs to create an engraved or stamped UIN tag. Other questions here are: who would create and issue these? Who would attach them?

7. Relax requirements for flying licenses: may be made compulsory for drones above 2 kg category and for operating above 120 m flying altitude as practiced in other countries. Also, the pilot license should be given after clearing ‖approved training courses‖ or endorsements available from approved training providers. More important is that such licensed pilots should come with additional privileges and they should not require any further approvals except for public liability insurance.

Outlook

The further development of drones and their integration in non-segregated airspace will pose new challenges. While today flying a single drone in non-segregated airspace with cooperative aircraft can be done with appropriate coordination and special procedures, the operation of several drones possibly with non-cooperative aircraft will be much more complicated and will require additional measures. However, the recent display of an array of 150 drones during the concluding session of the Kumbh, world's largest congregation of well over a million people at the confluence of the Ganga and Yamuna rivers at Allahabad, demonstrates that we do have sound safety measures in place for operating drones in non-segregated airspace.

In a country like India, the potential of drone application for scientific as well as commercial sector is enormous and the technical expertise to handle this challenge has been steadily growing. There seems to be a general acceptance and willingness in the government and private sectors to use this powerful technology for public use for various reasons—cost of operation, data quality, ease of data collection and repeatability. Therefore, simplifying the regulations for drone operations and streamlining the process for obtaining the necessary clearance for safe and effective use of drones makes a lot of sense and this could deliver huge benefits for the country.

Government of India's Ministry of Civil Aviation announced guidelines for remotely piloted aircraft — or drones as they are more commonly known — which will come into effect from 1 December 2018, aiming to open up an array of opportunities in the Indian civil aviation sector. Unveiling the "Drone Regulations 1.0" in New Delhi, Civil Aviation Minister Suresh Prabhu said that the guidelines would help foster technology and innovation in the development of drones — devices which have an extensive range of applications ranging from disaster relief to agriculture. "The drone market in India holds the potential of hitting over $1 trillion. We plan to develop drone manufacturing not only for the domestic market but abroad as well," Prabhu said, adding that India's expertise in technology is characterised by its capacity to devise low-cost solutions. The minister said that these drone regulations had taken so long to be formed because of various safety and security issues that needed to be sorted out.

His ministry, however, stated three specific reasons for these regulations to have taken so long to be formulated:

1. Drone technologies have been evolving very rapidly.
2. Many countries are still experimenting with their drone regulations and no ICAO (International Civil Aviation Organization) stands have been developed.
3. India's security environment necessitates extra precautions.

Minister of State for Civil Aviation Jayant Sinha said that Drone Regulations 1.0 have been formulated as an "all digital process" that will become effective from 1 December, which is when the "Digital Sky" platform will become operative.

Here's everything you need to know about the new government regulations for drones:

'All-digital platform'

As Sinha also pointed out, the new Digital Sky platform will be the first-of-its-kind national unmanned traffic management (UTM) platform that implements a 'no permission, no takeoff' system for remotely piloted aircraft. Users will be required to make one-time registration of their drones, pilots and owners on the platform, which will also allow for online filing of a drone's specific flight path and use.

"For every flight, users will be required to ask for permission to fly on a mobile app and an automated process permits or denies the request instantly. To prevent unauthorized flights and to ensure public safety, any drone without a digital permit to fly will simply not be able to takeoff," the ministry said.

The UTM platform operates as a traffic regulator in the drone airspace and coordinates closely with the defence and civilian air traffic controllers (ATCs) to ensure that drones remain on approved flight paths.

"The regulations are intended to enable visual line-of-sight, daytime-only and a maximum of 400-feet altitude flight operations," Sinha said. These limitations are not likely to last very long, as a committee called the Drone Task Force will work to expand the Indian regulations to meet global standards.

The Drone Task Force

A Drone Task Force, under the chairmanship of Sinha, will provide draft recommendations for the next series of regulations — the Drone Regulations 2.0. According to the ministry, these upcoming regulations will deal with, among other things, the following issues:
1. Certification of safe and controlled operation of drone hardware and software
2. Airspace management through automated operations linked into overall airspace management framework
3. Beyond visual-line-of-sight operations
4. Contribution to establishing global standards.
5. Suggestions for modifications of existing CARs (civil aviation requirements) and/or new CARs.

Operational requirements

The new regulations have categorized drones into five separate types, on the basis of their weight. The rules that apply for the drones will depend on the weight class that they fall into, which begin from under 250 grams and extend to over 150 kilograms. The five types are nano, micro, small, medium and large.

Other than nano, all other categories of drones need to be registered with the government and issued with a Unique Identification Number (UIN). Drones owed by central intelligence agencies do not have this requirement as well, not surprisingly.

Beyond these permissions, an Unmanned Aircraft Operator Permit (UAOP) is also required for drone operators, except for nano-drones operating below 50 feet and micro-drones operating below 200 feet.

Airspace, too, has been divided by the government into different zones. Here's what they indicate:
1. **Red Zone:** Flying not permitted
2. **Yellow Zone:** Controlled airspace permission required before flying
3. **Green Zone:** Uncontrolled airspace automatic permission

Beyond these, there are also specific regions around the country that have been marked as 'No Drone Zones'. Some of these No Drone Zones that have been defined are areas around airports, those near the international border, Vijay Chowk in New Delhi, State Secretariat Complex in state capitals and what the ministry called "strategic locations/vital and military installations". As of now, drones are allowed to operate within visual line of sight, during daytime only, and up to a maximum altitude of 400 feet. The FAQs released by the ministry also specify that delivery of items using drones is "not allowed as of now". Government agencies, however, can use drones for making deliveries, Sinha said.

Necessary equipment on board

The mandatory equipment required for operation of drones except those which fall into the nano category are:
1. GNSS -Global Navigation Satellite System
2. Return-To-Home (RTH) feature
3. Anti-collision light
4. ID-Plate
5. Flight controller with flight data logging capability
6. Radio Frequency ID and SIM/ No-Permission No Take off (NPNT)

To deal with non-compliance

In addition to the multiple checks and balances put in place for drone operators, the government will also enforce punitive action against those who do not comply with these new regulations after 1 December 2018.
1. The following enforcement actions have been stated by the civil aviation ministry
2. Suspension or cancellation of UIN/ UAOP in case of violation of regulatory provisions
3. Actions as per relevant Sections of the Aircraft Act 1934, or Aircraft Rules, or any statutory provisions

4. Penalties as per applicable sections in the Indian Penal Code (such as 287, 336, 337, 338, or other relevant sections in the IPC)

'New chapter in Indian aviation'

Hailing the list of government regulations for drones, Prabhu said, "Today we start an exciting new chapter in India's aviation history by allowing commercial use of drones. I am sure that many new and exciting applications will emerge that will propel India's economy forward. Our progressive regulations will encourage a vast Made in India drone industry."

His deputy, Sinha, believes that these regulations will place the country among the global leaders in drone technology. He said, "We want to establish a world-leading drone ecosystem. These regulations firmly place us among the global leaders. Our policy roadmap will certainly provide a strong impetus to all players in the drone ecosystem. We hope that these initiatives will enable unto create a vibrant new industry."

GLOBAL GOVERNANCE OF DRONES

Given the growing demand for drones especially in the non-military sector, the need for policies and regulations has become more urgent. Thousands of drones and UAVs are already in use in many developed countries and yet governments and multilateral organisations have not developed a framework regulating this sector. The UAV landscape is changing much faster than the governments' ability to keep up with the changes. The net result is a policy void.

Global Governance

Globally, rules and regulations around the use of drones are still in its infancy. Even though India is still a small player as compared to the US and China, New Delhi could take the initiative in framing rules of global governance partly because the evolution of drone technology could have serious security implications for India, but equally because it is better 32 for India to lead the initiative and protect its interests.

So far, at the multilateral level, the International Civil Aviation Organisation (ICAO) is the lead platform for framing rules of the road GLOBAL GOVERNANCE OF DRONES: GUIDELINES, REGULATIONS, AND POLICY GAPS IN INDIA 20 ORF OCCASIONAL PAPER # 145 MARCH 2018 for drone operations. Although it began its work on UAVs back in 2007, the first set of rules in the form of Circular 328 was issued only in 2011. Subsequently, it developed the Remotely Piloted Aircraft Systems (RPAS) Manual. Circular 328 became the first step towards regulating the sector.

It called on –states to provide comments, _particularly with respect to its [drone] application and usefulness‘‖ with the aim of developing _the fundamental international regulatory framework through Standards and Recommended Practices (SARPs), with supporting Procedures for Air Navigation Services (PANS) and guidance material, to underpin routine operation of UAS throughout the world in a safe, harmonized and seamless manner comparable to that of manned 33 operations.‘‖ However, the more comprehensive set of standards and regulations is set to be promulgated in 2018. Currently, the ICAO in addition to the Circular has amended three UAS-related amendments to its Annexes – Amendment 13 to Annex 13: Defining accident to include reference to unmanned aircraft (March 2010), Amendment 6 to Annex 7: Registration and identification requirements for remotely piloted aircraft (April 2012) and Amendment 43 to Annex 2: High level requirements relating to remotely piloted aircraft systems (April 2012). The ICAO must also look at best practices from other countries that could be added to the bask ORF OCCASIONAL PAPER # 145 MARCH 2018 21 before it is formalised into a law.

The more dynamic aspect of the proposal is that it has been developed in consultation with members of drone industry, UAV operators, aviation representatives and aero modeling associations, in addition to all the EASA member states. Even as EASA firms up the proposal into a law, it is the responsibility of individual member countries to set more operational restrictions such as air space limitations, in terms of, for instance, how many kilometers above the ground they can operate. Different European countries have different regulations for instance; one can fly drones commercially in Switzerland if line-of-sight can be ensured, within certain altitude limitations and not flying near protected areas such as airports. On the other hand, France has somewhat more restrictive regulations in place and it is mandated that any drone operation over the city of Paris needs to be authorised by aviation authorities.

US Regulations:

The US has by far the most commercial-friendly regulations in place. The New Small UAS Rule (107) of the Federal Aviation Administration (FAA) that came into existence in August 2016 regulates most operations of 37 drones, especially those that fall under commercial or work purposes. Part 107 rules specifies that an operator can apply for a waiver of Part 107 rule if the drone weighs less than 55 lbs, however, the waiver application must specifically state how the operator plans to safely conduct the operation, including emergency risk mitigation strategies. Drones weighing 0.55 lbs to 55 lbs must be registered with the FAA and most significantly, the UAV must be within the visual line-of-sight.

The line of-sight principle is not particularly pleasing to the industry and it is of the view that rules could become further relaxed once the sector reaches full automation. The FAA is believed to have relaxed the rules for drone operations in the commercial sector keeping in mind that the drone applications are estimated to generate an additional US$82 bn to the US 38 economies. Many industry giants including DJI Innovations (China DRONES: GUIDELINES, REGULATIONS, AND POLICY GAPS IN INDIA 22 ORF OCCASIONAL PAPER # 145 MARCH 2018 headquartered (Dajiang), the world's largest drone manufacturer, Pix4D attest to this potential. For UAV operations other than for work or commercial purposes, and specifically for recreational activities and hobbies, there are specific laws such as Public Law 112-95 Section 336 which states that UAVs must operate within visual line-of-sight, give way to manned aircraft, provide advance notification to the airport and air traffic control tower, when flying within five miles of an airport, and 39 also the UAV must not weigh more than 55 lbs.

Regulations in Australia

Australia was one of the first few countries to establish a regulatory framework in the area of drones, with the first set of regulations coming 40 out as early as in 2002. The Australian Civil Aviation Safety Authority has the primary responsibility of ensuring safety and regulating drone operations under different categories such as drone operations for fun, 41 hobbies or commercial ventures. New rules regulating drone operations were issued in September 2016, which have been framed 42 particularly from a risk-reduction and safety perspective. The new regulations accordingly are meant to be less restrictive from a legal and regulatory perspective, thereby facilitating low-risk operations.

The new rules also exempt small commercial drone operators from paying the US$1,400 in regulatory fees as well as avoid the lengthy documentation and paper work. Also, property holders are allowed to operate drones up to 25 kg on their properties without any approval. There are still grey areas that require more clarity in the regulation. For instance, a drone operation that does not seek any ‒commercial gain‖ can operate without any certification but the concept of ‒commercial gain‖ can be interpreted in multiple ways. If an operator is using UAVs to advertise a product or if an operator seeks to shoot videos and upload onto YouTube, these may not see a direct commercial benefit but they go 43 to publicize a certain industry or an activity

Japan's Drone Regulations:

Japan came up with its first set of regulations only after a serious incident where a small drone was found on the roof of the prime 44 minister's office building in Tokyo in April 2015. The incident brought about the urgency to regulate drone use and, accordingly, the ruling Liberal Democratic Party (LDP) proposed a bill to the Diet (Japanese Parliament) in June 2015. A separate bill, which proposed amendments to the Aviation Act was submitted in July 2015 and both the bills were 45 passed in the Diet subsequently.

Under the new regulations, an operator can fly a UAV only after obtaining permission from the Ministry of Land, Infrastructure and Transportation (MLIT) where there is air traffic such as airports and other approach areas, or areas above 150 metres. There are also restrictions for drone use in the hours of dawn and dusk, in addition to the requirement to maintain more than 30 metres of distance from people and objects. Violations are subjected 46 to a fine of upto (US$4,000 approximate) 500,000 yen. Japan's regulations relating to drones have been drawn, keeping in view the function of drones in the commercial context. Nevertheless, terrorism and other security-related concerns have pushed for stronger regulations for drones for hobby and recreational activities.

China's Regulatory Framework:

China has in recent years emerged as a major hub for manufacturing of drones. Some of the industry majors in drones such as DJI (Dajiang) Innovations, Zero Zero Robotics, Yuneec, and Hubsan belong to China. Five out of 11 global venture-capital funded drone companies are in China and foreign companies are beginning to have a larger presence in 47 the country. China's use of drones for commercial purposes including in agriculture is likely to pick up greater momentum, even as the legal and regulatory architecture is yet to be clearly defined. Also, there are safety issues that need to be dealt with.

In December 2015, the online DRONES: GUIDELINES, REGULATIONS, AND POLICY GAPS IN INDIA 24 ORF OCCASIONAL PAPER # 145 MARCH 2018 commercial giant Alibaba's drone out on a test crashed into a landing 48 military jet, demonstrating the safety issues that arc far from settled.

Current regulations, as they exist today, differ across regions—Beijing and Shanghai appear to have far stricter policies regarding when and where drones can be flown – given the densely populated nature of these cities. Regulations also make a distinction between small consumer drones and large commercial-use drones. Following a series of accidents involving drones, the Civil Aviation Administration of China (CAAC) began putting in place stricter laws in June 2017 that mandate civilian drones above a certain size to be registered under real names in 49 order to strengthen the safety measures associated with use of drones. China's lead role in the drone market and the potential for large-scale use of drones in commercial and non-commercial sectors are significant but the regulatory and legal frameworks are yet to take firm roots.

*****

Chapter-4

Drones Transforming Media Industry

Drones can be used for journalism, alongside many other civilian purposes. Ethical considerations such as safety and privacy are likely to arise in the context of drone journalism. This raises pertinent questions of whether journalists can use drones at all and whether capturing pictures in public places by drones is permissible under Indian law.

Drone technology is now entering newsrooms. Some news agencies in India have deployed drones for the 2014 election coverage and journalism students at the University of Missouri are studying _Drone reporting' in their curriculum. They can be used for taking images as well as live video and other necessary data, at minimal cost. They provide safety to journalists by possibly replacing manned aircraft for reporting in hazardous, violent or calamity-affected areas. From sports events to election rallies, drones can provide better visual effects than traditional technology.

Drone technology has been used by defense organizations and tech-savvy consumers for quite some time. However, the benefits of this technology extend well beyond just these sectors. With the rising accessibility of drones, many of the most dangerous and high-paying jobs within the commercial sector are ripe for displacement by drone technology. The use cases for safe, cost-effective solutions range from data collection to delivery. And as autonomy and collision-avoidance technologies improve, so too will drones' ability to perform increasingly complex tasks.

A drone or a UAV (unmanned aerial vehicle) typically refers to a pilotless aircraft that operates through a combination of technologies, including computer vision, artificial intelligence, object avoidance tech, and others. But drones can also be ground or sea vehicles that operate autonomously.

The use of drones is transforming the media industry – for example, action sequences in movies can now be taken from an aerial view smoothly, journalists can cover news in areas where human entry could be dangerous or prohibited, photographers can click dream pictures of places in nature which may otherwise be inaccessible, etc.

Drones in media are being used mainly:

1. To film movies and television serials
2. To cover news footage in journalism
3. To record events and functions
4. For Aerial Photography

Filming Movies and Television Serials:

Cinematographers today are using the Drone technology to capture those stunning panoramas and actions that you witness sitting in your living room. Movies like the Expendables 3, Transformers: Age of Extinction, The Wolf of Wall Street, and Captain America were shot using drones to provide a real-life experience to the viewers. Drones are being used for filming shots that require adrenalin-filled action sequences, literal birds' eye views, dramatic panoramas or 360-degree views of subjects. No other filming method can start a sequence inside a building and end up at 400 feet altitude in one uncut shot. Not only do drones allow to build a better mental picture of the layout of the land, but it can also get down to ground level, with smaller shadows and less air disturbance, unlike helicopters.

Journalism Industry:

Due to the increasing capabilities of drones, their popularity has risen to high levels, particularly in journalism and filming documentaries. The impact of the Syrian Civil War on Aleppo was captured using drone footage by the New York Times. A news story comes to life when the viewers get to see the journalist moving towards the prohibited or dangerous area to cover the action live on the ground and in real time. This not only increases the footage clarity but also the credibility of the news being provided by the channel.

Aerial Photography:

Drones have propelled the art of photography and videography to fantastic new heights. They have opened up a myriad of possibilities for photographers, videographers, and casual hobbyists alike.

The most attractive draw of using a drone for photography is that it allows you to shoot from a higher perspective. This can instantly transform plain old photos into something truly spectacular. Drones have built-in cameras that can rotate and swivel to allow the operator to shoot photos and videos from all sorts of angles. This is especially useful for photographers, as it can provide them with more freedom in creating the perfect photo.

Nature and wildlife photographers no longer need to go on perilous treks through jungles and rainforests or hike up steep mountains to take photos. Photojournalists no longer need to place themselves in the middle of disaster areas and war zones. With the help of drones, photographers have the option of documenting subjects and events in inaccessible locations.

The New York Times made extensive use of drones in media coverage and highlighted how the new technology made this reporting possible. A story on the impact of the Syrian Civil War on Aleppo captured using drone footage was featured on the front page, and, realizing the impact drones had on coverage, the newspaper put together a list of top stories it told through drone footage across the world.

CNN launched a team dedicated to flying and operating drones as part of expanded news coverage. The news network used drones as a way of augmenting its traditional television coverage, providing the benefits of traditional aerial vehicles such as planes and helicopters, and the improved vantage point they can provide, but for a fraction of the cost.

Drones were also the cause of governmental action, with police and local authorities imposing no-fly zones to forestall the possibility of media coverage using drones. During civil unrest in 2014 in Ferguson, MI, police requested that airspace be closed off to prevent media from gathering footage. Similarly, authority's instituted no-fly zones in the vicinity of protests at Standing Rock, ND, which protestors and journalists claimed was to prevent coverage of the protests and the acts of police.

Using drones is already transforming the media, and that will only increase as drones become more widespread and technically able. As authorities are forced to create regulations that permit more widespread use of drones, this trend will only increase moving forward. Drones are not just toys, but enterprise tools as well as part of a new wave in media.

Drones turned the corner in 2015 to become a popular consumer device, while a framework for regulation that legitimizes drones in the US began to take shape. Technological and regulatory barriers still exist to further drone adoption.

Drone technology for commercial purposes across industries:

1. Defense

While drones have been used by the military for over a decade (the Predator UAV is among the most well known), smaller, portable drones are now being used by ground forces on a regular basis. Military spending for this technology is expected to grow as an overall percentage of large military budgets such as the United States' $640B defense budget, offering specialized drone manufacturers and software developers a tremendous opportunity.

Many of the drones are being designed exclusively for surveillance, but others for offensive operations.

Prox Dynamics, a military grade UAV manufacturer acquired by FLIR Systems in Q4'16, has become one of the many reconnaissance UAVs used by militaries around the world, including the US Marines, the British Army, the Australian Army, and Norway's Armed Forces. In addition to the use of new aerial technologies, militaries continue to use unmanned ground vehicles, or UGVs, to lead tactical initiatives. Startup Clearpath Robotics manufactures both UAVs and UGVs and lists the US Department of Defense, the US Army, and the US Navy as clients.

2. Emergency Response

Innovations in camera technology have had significant impacts on the growing use of drones. UAVs outfitted with thermal imaging cameras have provided emergency response teams with an ideal solution for identifying victims who are difficult to spot with the naked eye. In 2017, Land Rover partnered with the Austrian Red Cross to design a special operations vehicle with a roof-mounted, thermal imaging drone.

The vehicle includes an integrated landing system, which allows the drone to securely land atop the vehicle while in motion. This custom Land Rover Discovery, dubbed –Project Hero,‖ hopes to save lives by speeding up response times. Startup companies and universities are also designing systems intended for search and rescue. Flyability, developer of a collision-tolerant

UAV, has performed particularly well in confined areas with limited lines of sight environments often encountered by emergency response teams.

Additionally, Delft University of Technology has tested an ambulance drone that could deliver defibrillators on demand. By extending existing emergency infrastructure, drones may be able to dramatically increase survival rates in both rural and urban areas around the world.

3. Humanitarian Aid & Disaster Relief

In addition to emergency response, drones have proved useful during times of natural disaster. In the aftermath of hurricanes and earthquakes, UAVs have been used to assess damage, locate victims, and deliver aid. And in certain circumstances, they are being used to prevent disasters altogether. To help monitor and combat forest fires, surveillance drones outfitted with thermal imaging cameras are being deployed to detect abnormal forest temperatures. By doing so, teams are able to identify areas most prone to forest fires or identify fires just 3 minutes after they begin. While recreational drones are strictly prohibited in active forest fire regions, they have proved useful when operated by the appropriate teams.

4. Conservation

Poaching and climate change have a dramatic impact on the health of wildlife worldwide. Fortunately, conservationists are adopting innovative methods to protect and study our global ecosystems. In combination with geospatial imagery, drones are now used to monitor and track animals, while UAVs are also used to tag animals and collect samples. DJI Innovations has been a leader within the conservation space, allowing teams to conduct research without disturbing natural habitats. The Ocean Alliance is an example of an organization that has used drones (such as the marine Snot Bot) to collect samples specifically, mucus from whales. In addition to facilitating research on ecosystems, drones can also allow conservationists to track and incarcerate poachers.

5. Disease Control

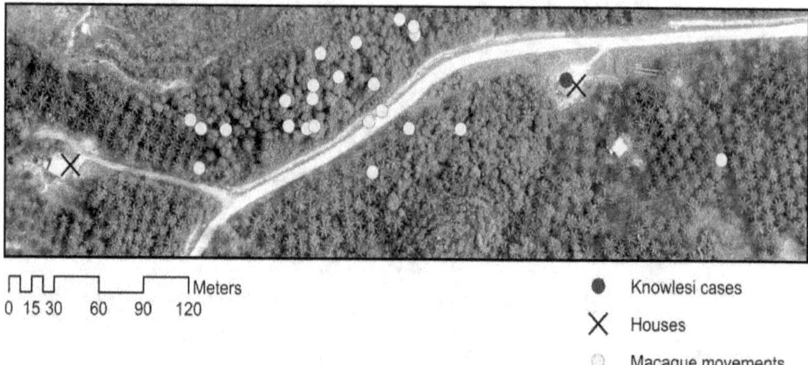

Tracking animals also allows researchers to track disease. Drones with thermal imaging cameras have been used by the London School of Hygiene and Tropical Medicine to track macaque movements in the province of Palawan in the Philippines — a region where malaria is an active threat.

The ability to follow these animals provided further insight into the possible movement of infectious disease and its jumps from animals to humans. In a similar vein, Microsoft is also leveraging drone technology to capture and test mosquitoes for infectious disease. Ideally, this intelligence could be used to protect local residents, and in the future could be used to prevent epidemics before they begin.

6. Healthcare

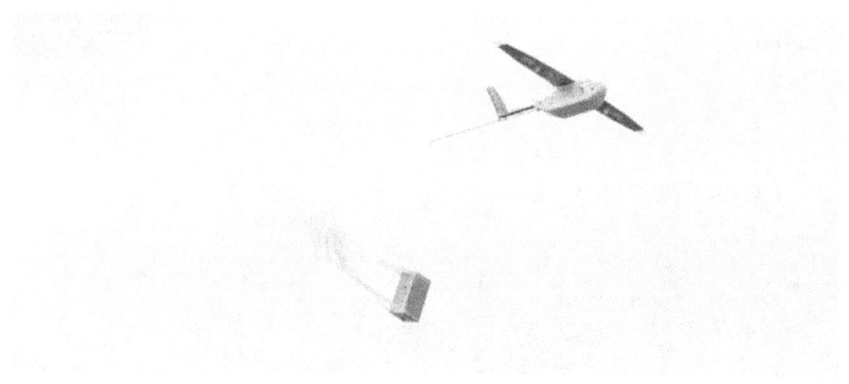

Modern medicine has had a profound impact on preventing disease, increasing life expectancy, and raising general standards of living. However, access to modern medicine has been rather difficult in many rural regions around the world. While medical supplies can be delivered by traditional means, certain circumstances call for quick access to drugs, blood, and medical technology — a need drones could fill. One of the most prominent venture-backed medical delivery companies is Zipline International. Zipline has launched delivery drones in rural areas throughout Africa and continues to expand its reach. Flirtey drones have also been used to deliver medicine.

7. Agriculture

Intrinsically, our health is tied to the food we eat, with agriculture playing an important role in our well-being. Additionally, farmers are striving to reduce costs and expand yields. With the use of drones, agricultural workers are able to gather data, automate redundant processes, and generally maximize efficiency. Raptor Maps, a leader in agricultural analytics, relies on drones to help farmers better understand their potential harvest. After cultivating healthy crops, the process of harvesting is repetitive, time-consuming, and detail oriented. To address this, equipment manufacturer Case IH has built an autonomous tractor, while Abundant Robotics is developing a solution for autonomously picking produce. Planting crops can be an equally tedious and energy-intensive process, but companies like Drone

Seed are tackling this problem at 350 feet per second. In a research capacity, drones have also been used to pollinate flowers, and could one day prove helpful in compensating for the declining bee population.

8. Weather Forecasting

As climate change continues, scientists are leveraging new forms of hardware and software for data collection. Today, most data is collected through stationary structures or captured with geospatial imaging solutions. Drones, however, offer a versatile solution that can physically follow weather patterns as they develop. In addition to aerial vehicles, unmanned surface vehicles (USVs) are changing the way data is gathered. Saildrone has developed an autonomous sailboat that collects oceanic and atmospheric data from the ocean surface. The data collected has been used to better understand our environment and imminent weather trends. Atmosar gathers and analyzes weather data to maximize UAV flight duration and stability.

9. Maritime

Navigating oceans and ports requires an immense amount of expertise and labor from the estimated 1.65 million people serving on international merchant ships today. But with increasing amounts of oceanic data and innovations in autonomy, unmanned marine vehicles could become the standard for maritime shipping. Rolls-Royce has already completed a number of trials with unmanned vessels controlled remotely. Inspecting ships is also an important and regular part of the industry. While Rolls-Royce plans to use smaller UAVs to inspect ships above the surface, Orobotix has designed an underwater drone used to inspect hulls from below.

10. Waste Management

Recycling and biodegradation have dramatically improved global waste management. However, innovations in waste collection are still emerging. Fortunately, drones operate at the forefront of these initiatives and have helped to clean our oceans. RanMarine operates a Roomba-like unmanned marine vehicle used to collect waste in ports and harbors, while Red Zone Robotics focuses exclusively on wastewater management.

11. Energy

While alternative energy has become increasingly popular, fossil fuels still remain the world's primary energy source. Inspection of the infrastructure used to extract, refine, and transport oil and gas is an important aspect of the industry. Regulation requires certain standards to minimize the risk of environmental damage.

With the use of drones, much of this inspection work can be done remotely and safely. Sky-Futures is a UAV company focused on oil and gas inspection, and is used by many of the world's largest oil companies to inspect offshore rigs. SkyX Systems also focuses on oil and gas inspections, but specializes in pipeline assessment. Cyberhawk Innovations, meanwhile, offers solutions for both fossil fuel energy and alternative energy providers.

12. MINING

Mining is a capital-intensive venture that requires constant measurement and assessment of physical material. Stockpiles of ore or rock or minerals are difficult to measure. But with unique cameras, drones are able to capture volumetric data on stockpiles and survey mining operations from the air. This reduces the risks associated with having surveyors on the ground.

Airobotics provides an industrial grade on-site drone solution used by mining companies for measuring materials, surveying operations, and general security. The system is fully autonomous and stored in on-site housing that can autonomically swap cameras and batteries.

Mining is also being disrupted by autonomous vehicles, such as the unmanned ground vehicle (UGV) designed by Komatsu. Similar to many other drones today, these vehicles can be controlled remotely without a line of sight needed.

13. Construction Planning

One of the most popular commercial use cases for drones is construction planning and management. Software developers have created solutions that analyze construction progress with regularly captured data. While ground surveying is still a critical part of construction planning and monitoring, the use of drone data has become increasingly important.

Camera technology is used to monitor buildings and gauge topography and soil type throughout the construction lifecycle. Skycatch offers these solutions in a monthly software subscription. Their software can pair with a self-manufactured Skycatch UAV, or with a number of DJI drones. Dronomy offers a similar suite of software solutions intended to enhance project monitoring and site management.

14. Infrastructure Development

While drones serve a useful and immediate purpose in construction planning and management, they also have the potential to be used to develop physical infrastructure.

ETH Zürich, a university in Switzerland, partnered with roboticist Raffaello D'Andrea and architecture firm Gramazio Kohler Architects to create a structure built entirely by UAVs.

By programming the drones to lift and stack thousands of polymer bricks, the team was able to create a geometric structure nearly 10 meters high. The finished product serves as a concept for a ‒vertical village‖ that would employ a similar structure, which would be built by larger drones.

15. Insurance

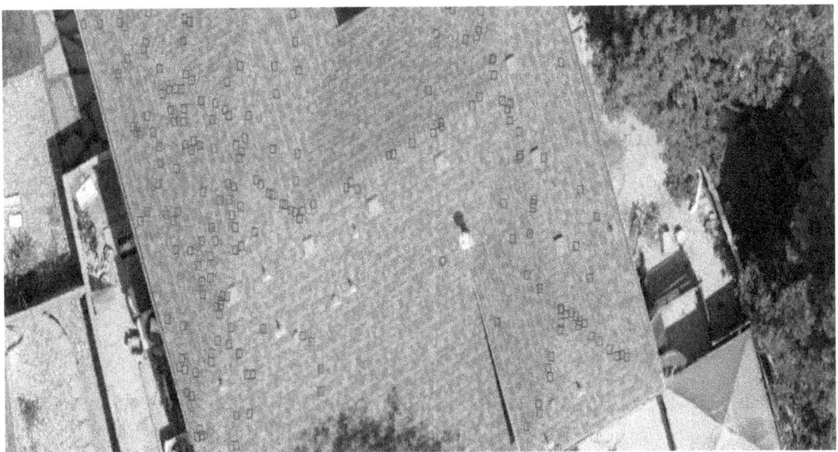

Insurance inspections are a core area where insurance companies can leverage drones. Traditionally, inspectors and assessors for property insurance would scale structures to conduct manual inspections of properties, but now drones can provide an equally detailed assessment with high-resolution cameras.

While damaged or defective property still requires the attention of a physical inspection, UAVs are beginning to have an impact there as well.

Drone companies focused on the insurance industry include Converge Industries, which has helped ease the work of insurance inspectors, and Kespry, which has partnered with Farmers Insurance to scale its offerings in the space.

16. Realty

Drones have been beneficial in capturing pictures of high-value properties, showing that even the real estate industry can be upended by drone technology. Drone Base offers on-demand photography solutions (among others) for a number of different industries, including residential and commercial real estate.

While low-cost aerial photography is being leveraged to take images of a property's exterior, home interiors are also being captured by small, agile UAVs. Zaw Studios, a media company based outside of Los Angeles, uses drones to capture immersive 360-degree photographs and videos within large homes. The finished product provides potential buyers with a perspective that replicates a physical walk-through.

17. Urban Planning

As urbanization continues, cities have to adapt to larger populations and chronic congestion. Urban planning has become increasingly important for cities, but requires a thorough understanding of metropolitan rhythms and flows. With the use of drones, urban planners are able to better understand their environments and implement data-driven improvements.

Engineering consulting firm Arup has used drones to gather data in population-dense areas, allowing users to better understand their urban habitat. With many municipalities on limited budgets, drones notably provide a low-cost way to capture invaluable urban data. Specifically, drones have helped city planners determine which areas may benefit most from green space, without causing further congestion.

18. Personal Transportation

While our definition of drones is typically limited to unmanned vehicles, certain forms of autonomous transportation should be considered drone transportation. For example, EHANG has built an autonomous aerial vehicle (AAV), which operates with four rotors (quadcopter) for vertical takeoff. The vehicle can transport passengers between destinations, even in an urban environment with plenty of obstacles. The AAV requires minimal passenger input and incorporates fail-safe functionality or built-in systems for safe landings in case of engine failure or collision.

Lilium Aviation also looks to build an autonomous aerial vehicle for passenger transportation, but leverages a design more comparable to a Harrier Jet or F-35 than a quadcopter drone.

19. Airlines

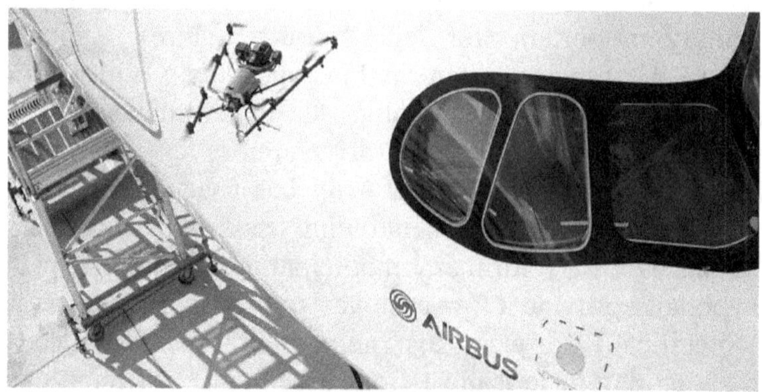

Compliance is a challenge for many industries, but the airline industry must adhere to particularly stringent levels of regulatory standards. FAA inspections vary in comprehensiveness, but basic inspections are conducted after every 125 hours of flight time. Additionally, airlines are expected to conduct their own routine inspections before every flight.

In an attempt to improve this process, Intel partnered with Airbus to conduct exterior aircraft inspections with UAVs. Intel supplied the drones (gained through their acquisition of Ascending Technologies in 2016), which are outfitted with cameras that allow them to collect images and data that can be used to create detailed, 3D-models of the Airbus fleet.

Airbus has also launched its own drone subsidiary called Airbus Aerial, which looks to provide inspection solutions across a variety of industries. Canard Drones, meanwhile, provides inspection solutions for airports rather than aircrafts.

20. Telecommunications

Telecommunication towers also are inspected frequently to ensure service reliability. In the aftermath of Hurricane Harvey, AT&T and Verizon launched drones in Houston, Texas to inspect their towers a process which would have been too dangerous and time-consuming to do manually. These drones were able to quickly assess damage so that repair teams could be deployed to restore service. In many cases, service was restored in hours rather than days.

Skyward, an inspection drone company purchased by Verizon in Q1'17, provides a Drone-as-a-Service software platform that helps commercial drone operators in a variety of industries. Given a recent run of natural disasters, this proved to be a particularly beneficial acquisition for Verizon.

21. Internet Access

With the world's largest technology firms vying for our time and attention, the need for global internet access is becoming more and more central to business models.

Facebook experimented with a solar-powered drone called Aquila, which planned to provide internet access to rural parts of the world. Aquila was a core component of Facebook's Internet.org initiative before stopping development in mid-2018.

Google initially acquired solar-powered drone company Titan Aerospace to provide UAV-powered internet (similar to Aquila), but the venture proved challenging. They have since pivoted toward a weather balloon-like design (Project Loon) that will provide internet access from the stratosphere.

22. The Outdoor Industry

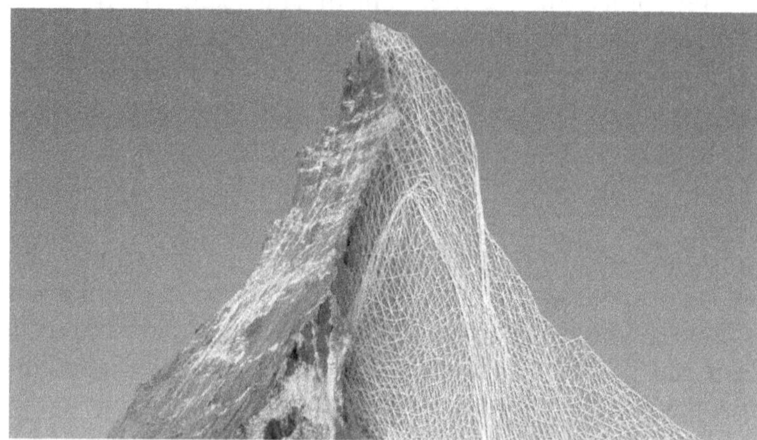

In the consumer area, an early application for drones was as a recreational tool for the great outdoors. Between aerial landscape photography and extreme sports footage, UAVs changed the way people experienced the planet.

Today, drones are being used for more than breathtaking photos and award-winning film. Sense Fly, acquired by Parrot in Q3'12, has had its drones used to create a 3D rendering of the infamous Matterhorn peak in Zermatt, Switzerland. Drones were able to map the entire mountain face in less than 7 hours. These types of models are used by climbers and skiers to better understand the terrain.

23. Tourism & Hospitality

Not only have drones transformed the way hotels conduct marketing, but they may also transform our notion of luxury accommodations. Design firm HOK envisions drone hotels that can travel to unique locations on demand. These modern structures could fly to remote and traditionally inaccessible locations for guests. Traditional hotels are also adopting drones, such as Unsupervised AI, which uses drones to deliver packages and room service quickly and autonomously.

24. Live Entertainment

Drones have already had an impact on event surveillance and event photography/film, but are also being used more directly to entertain. Disney has been one of the more active companies in this space, and has filed for a number of drone patents focused on entertainment. Synchronized lights shows, floating projection screens, and drone puppeteers have all been considered by the entertainment giant. Verge Aero is one example of a private player creating live, synchronized drone performances for audiences.

25. Sports

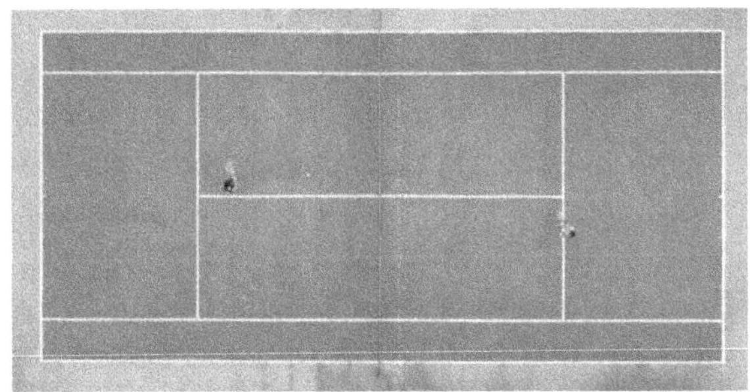

Skycam, a robotic camera suspended from a cable-driven, computerized transport system, changed the way viewers experience televised sports. The camera provides up-close and personal perspectives that traditional, stationary cameras cannot capture. Today, Skycam is a necessity for any professional arena sports broadcast. Drones, however, are becoming increasingly popular for professional sports outside of the stadium. Aero Cine (or Aerobo), for example, offers live sports broadcast services that have been used in a number of live and recorded TV broadcasts.

In addition to traditional sports, drones are influencing sports of their own. The Drone Racing League is a global drone-racing series that uses cutting-edge technologies to stream exciting content that can be shared with millions.

26. Hollywood

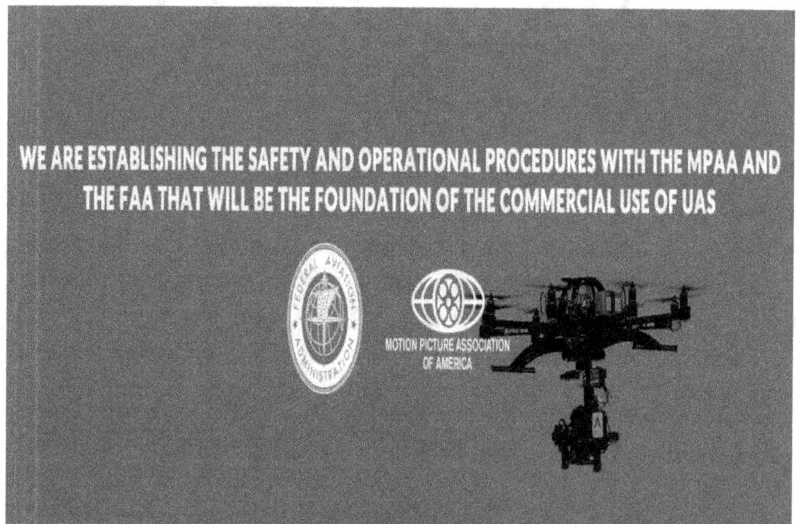

One of the first industries to adopt drones was professional film. Drones have allowed producers to capture dramatic aerial perspectives without the use of helicopters. This has had a dramatic impact on Hollywood's bottom line, pushing the limits in cinematography. As the adoption of this technology has grown, the FAA and MPAA have worked together to establish procedures for regulating commercial drone use within the space. Aerial MOB, acquired by 5D Robotics in Q2'16, has used drones to film content for movies like The Circle, Guardians of the Galaxy, and *La La Land*, among others. They have also used drones to film a variety of advertisements, including content for Apple Music.

27. Advertising

In addition to filming advertisements, drones are being used as physical mediums for marketing. They can power aerial advertising at live events or high traffic locations. Drone Cast has developed services for banner advertising and has delivered Ford-branded knickknacks to patrons at auto conventions. Hoovy.co, similarly, is focused on disrupting banner advertising.

28. Retail

Drones are being used to deliver goods from local retailers and fulfillment centers. Amazon is notorious for their innovations within the space and focus on fulfillment & logistics. The giant's patent activity related to drones is frequent and often newsworthy. Private markets are also flourishing with investment activity looking to increase both land and air delivery efficiency. Matternet has made efforts to combine delivery vans with aerial drones, while Starship Technologies is building a fleet of self-driving robots designed to deliver goods locally within 30 minutes

29. Manufacturing & Inventory Management

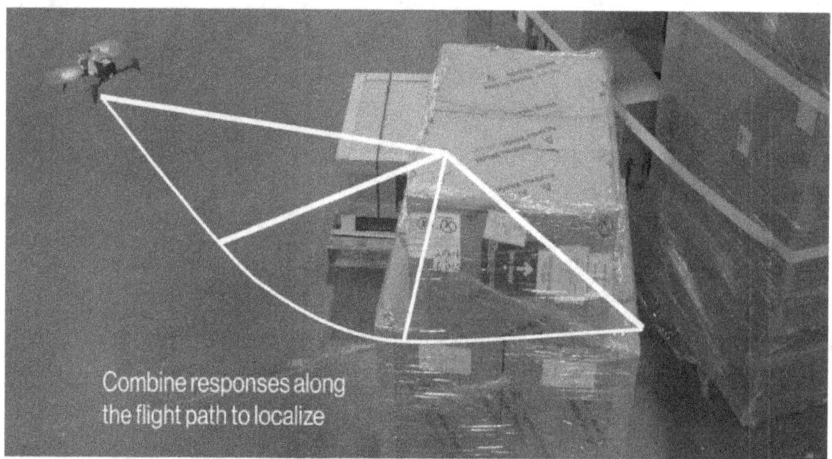

Robotics plays an essential role in today's assembly lines. And while drones may perform best in unstructured environments, they can nonetheless play a part in modern-day manufacturing. From raw material discovery to assembly line inspection, drones may take on tasks too difficult for large, pre-programmed robots and too dangerous or intricate for humans. In addition to manufacturing and delivery, drones can be used within warehouses and fulfillment centers for inventory management. Recent research out of MIT outlines an inventory system that leverages drones to communication with battery-free RFID technology. Drones could be used to locate and measure inventory within a network of individual sensors located on or in containers around the facility.

30. Underground Economies and Fighting Crime

Though drone technology has many positive uses, it has also been used to conduct illegal activities. In particular, drones have been used to transport drugs across international borders. Large drones, like DJI's Matrice 600, span nearly 5.5 feet and are designed to carry heavy Hollywood cameras. With flight times of 18 – 40 minutes (depending on the weight of payload) and top speeds of 40 mph, drones are ideal for transporting illicit cargo. On the flip side of the coin, drones are also used by law enforcement for surveillance and crime prevention.

31. Fitness

From wearables to 3D body scanning devices, fitness technology aims to make training and exercise regimens more personalized by tracking physical activity and biometrics. But to move from tracking to coaching, several new devices are emerging to provide feedback and guidance while users exercise. Drones could enhance the digital coaching experience by following users as they exercise and collecting video data of their workouts. There are already several consumer drones on the market that can be programmed to follow their owners, including FlyPro_s XEagle Sport drone, DJI_s Mavic Pro, and Ehang_s Ghostdrone 2.0.

For the visually impaired, drones could make exercise programs more accessible. In 2015, an associate professor of computer science at the University of Nevada, Reno's Human Plus Lab built a prototype drone that guides blind runners. The drone — which guides runners by sound is equipped with one camera that follows the lines around the track and one that focuses on a marker on the runner's shirt. It flies approximately 10 feet in front of the runner, and can adjust its speed to the runner's pace.

32. Food Services Industry

Online food ordering and delivery services are enabling fast casual restaurants to downsize their physical locations and lower real estate expenses, but delivery commission costs are still weighing down profits. Some restaurants are looking to use drones for faster, cheaper delivery.

Iceland-based AHA, an e-commerce platform with a food delivery feature similar to Grubhub, partnered with Israeli drone logistics company Flytrex in August 2017 to set up a small delivery route in Reykjavik. AHA and Flytrex use hexacopters to deliver food directly across a bay of the North Atlantic Ocean that delivery drivers normally have to circumvent, significantly cutting delivery time. The company plans to add more delivery routes in the future.

Drones seem to be gaining traction with pizza delivery, specifically. Domino's partnered with startup Flirtey in November 2016 to make the first-ever commercial pizza delivery by drone. The pie was dropped off to a couple in New Zealand. In 2018, HBO teamed up with brand delivery agency Fooji and Drone Dudes to send pizzas to fans of its show *Silicon Valley.*

Drones also have potential to change the way food is delivered inside the restaurant. In 2015, Infinium Robotics developed a drone waiter known as the Infinium-Serve to address Singapore's service staff shortage. The drones can carry up to 4.4 pounds of food and drink, which equates to about two pints of beer, two glasses of wine, and a whole pizza. Similarly, in 2016, a Dutch university opened a pop-up cafe that used drone waiters to take and deliver customer orders.

33. Journalism and News Coverage

News outlets are using drones to add context and understanding to news stories, enhance production value, and improve documentary storytelling.CNN reportedly has the most advanced drone program called CNN Air of any US news outlet. The network reports flying hundreds of missions in more than 20 countries. Footage collected by its drone fleet contributes to CNN's core news report, its Great Big Story initiative (dedicated to creating micro documentaries and short films), and other projects for Turner and Time Warner.

With drones, the crew can collect footage that would be difficult to get otherwise due to safety issues, high costs, and physical barriers. CNN's senior director of national news technology and aerial imagery & reporting Greg Agvent explains that drones allow the teams to –capture things that you simply cannot capture from a helicopter, which would create that much more noise and cost you that much more money.‖

CNN is currently working on leveraging data collected by its fleet to create digital models of areas the drones fly over. It also added body heat-detecting cameras to some of its drones to locate people using thermal imaging, and has plans to use virtual reality cameras and live graphics overlay in conjunction with its drones.

34. Air Travel

Airbus uses drones in routine plane inspections. The company captures data and images of its aircraft to help analyze the condition of the planes. But drones are influencing other aspects of air travel as well. Passengers traveling with drones must adhere to certain rules about storage of the devices' lithium-ion batteries and sharp components such as propellers. Rather than simply packing their drones into their suitcases, travelers need to educate themselves to safely and legally transport the machines.

Drones have created another set of safety concerns as well. In late December 2018, London's Gatwick airport closed for 36 hours due to drones flying nearby. British authorities said they believed whoever was flying the drones was deliberately interrupting flight traffic, which is against the law in England. Nonetheless, the challenge of identifying the person or persons behind the disruption highlights the difficulties of regulating drone activity more broadly.

35. Gaming

Drones now play a dual role in gaming as game components and as tools for developing them. The company Drone n Base sells gaming packages that allow players to wage drone races as well as engage in high-tech battles via augmented reality. Furthermore, the Aerial Sports League has been on the drone games scene since 2012. The company hosts drone combat and racing events, some of which offer significant monetary prizes.

Video game production companies are also using drone technology to develop hyper-realistic maps and other components for their games. Drones offer companies an opportunity to gain access to vast areas of terrain and outdoor elements that allow for richer, well-developed game visuals.

36. Space

NASA announced in May 2018 that a robocraft helicopter would be used in the Mars 2020 mission to find out whether there has ever been life on Mars. The helicopter will serve as a scout for the rover, gathering data about the planet's terrain and surveying areas the rover cannot reach. The small device (it weighs less than four pounds) is experimental, and if it proves useful during the mission, it could open the door to other aerial devices being used in space exploration.

37. Education

Drones may soon be popping up in classrooms, as educators embrace the potential for teaching a wide range of skills and supplementing more traditional lessons. For instance, math teachers might use drones to help students understand proportional relationships, while English teachers might jump-start kids' language skills by using drone photography to inspire writing exercises. Introducing these devices can create unique, tangible experiences that keep students engaged and retaining information in new ways.

38. Security

Security companies are using drones to provide more comprehensive surveillance systems for industrial, commercial, and residential properties. One company, Nightingale Security, enables clients to establish repeatable pathways that the drones can travel daily, monitoring key security areas. The same service deploys drones with live streaming capabilities immediately after an alarm is triggered, allowing the security team and clients to obtain key footage of a potential breach. Another business is exploring the use of drones in combination with sensors that would pick up potentially suspicious activity and then signal the aerial device to fly to that particular location.

Chapter- 5

Drone journalism scenario in World

Drones, as we know them today, represent a significant development in robotic technology and the private use of drones has started trending in media recently. The use of unmanned aircraft such as drones is not a new concept and the origins of the concept can be traced back to 1896, when the first pilotless steam-powered aircraft registered a powered flight lasting over one minute. Drones come in many shapes and sizes and can be operated by individuals for recreational or commercial purposes. Unlike traditional helicopters and hot air balloons, drones have the capability of flying at lower altitudes combined with data capturing capabilities of smart computing devices. They also differ from the traditional aircrafts, as they are mostly economical to operate and easily accessible to a wider range of population.

In common terminology, drones refer to aerial vehicles, which can fly without a human operator. For regulatory purposes, different countries and international organizations have provided varied definitions. Some of these definitions have been reproduced below. In general aviation and space-related parlance, a _Drone' refers to any vehicle that can operate on multiple surfaces and/or in the air without a human being on board to control it. They vary in size, shape, form, speed, and a host of other attributes, though some jurisdictions categorise and regulate them by weight. A drone could vary from a model aircraft / toy in a store or a large sized aircraft sent in a war zone.

Drones have multitude uses which have become apparent. They could be used for the quick delivery of donated organs, thereby avoiding the expense of hiring air transport or having to deal with traffic thereby potentially saving more lives. They can be used for enhancing agricultural efficiency by identifying factors such as moisture content and nutrient soil availability. Remote sensing through drones can be of significant use in disaster-prone areas like pinpointing and fighting fires or detection of theft and pilferage of goods meant for public utilization, or in detection of LPG gas leaks which can save several lives and resources.

Drones also find application in law and enforcement, helping with border patrolling, although cost concerns have been raised regarding a flagship effort on the US-Mexico border.18 However with improving technology such concerns can be overcome, and undeniable advantages such as being undetectable will help in preventing human and drug trafficking, spotting and reacting to border infractions and assistance in monitoring otherwise inaccessible terrain. One of the developments which have caught the imagination of the public has been drone delivery in e-commerce which was spearheaded by Amazon's announcement two years ago. This has however, run into problems with Federal Aviation Authority (FAA) regulations as discussed later.

The latest developments in the field include concepts such as _drone racing' which has garnered worldwide attention and a _drone taxi', where the passenger, would only set a flight plan and instruct the device to take off or land via a tablet, with no further controls. There would be a back-up control centre which may take over in an emergency. This drone, besides being a variation on the _flying car' theme is also characterized by its autonomy. The key issue here is the degree of autonomy that is granted to the non-human components. Many drones already have autonomous functionality, to the extent that they avoid collisions and some to the extent that there are only provided general instructions or waypoints to follow, with the rest being left up to the drone.

While regulations have generally not addressed this aspect, the circular released with the latest FAA regulations in June 2016, has allowed autonomous operation, but within certain limits. However, it does not provide for regulation over larger drones as in the case of a drone taxi or it having only non-pilot human passengers. While it remains in a legal grey area, this field is likely to evolve along the lines of self-driven cars.

Unauthorized surveillance

It is well known that drones can be easily utilized for mass surveillance. This is to be understood in context of digital technologies that aim to revolutionize our daily lives, by having more detailed records about those lives. In the name of national security and terrorism, surveillance mechanisms are utilized to track and profile the citizens by the state as well and private agencies. By the virtue of their design and size, drones can operate undetected, allowing the user to monitor people without their knowledge.

For instance, there are drones with super high resolution giga pixel cameras that can be used to track people and vehicles from altitudes as high as 20,000 feet. They can carry equipment such as fake towers, which can break Wi-Fi codes and intercept text messages & cell phone conversations without the knowledge of either the communication provider or the user. Drones equipped with advanced technologies can penetrate test networks and collect unencrypted data and even establish fake access points.

Such unwarranted surveillance casts chilling effects on the citizen's civil liberties, intellectual privacy eclipse people's right to dissent. Moreover, information collected surreptitiously can be used to blackmail or discredit opponents. Surveillance is not restricted to the state; in fact the private companies also generate vast fortunes from the collection, use and sale of personal data. Although it may be argued that the collection of data about a person does not violate her/ his privacy interests per se, extensive collection can rise to a level of privacy intrusion.

Take you on a ride to the world of journalism:

1. **Nepal earthquake 2015**

The Drone Journalism Society sent drones to Nepal post the devastating earthquake in March this year to collect data about the damage. This became a milestone in the world of journalism as for the first time in the history of journalism a 3D model was created about any damage caused by a natural disaster to help world organisations in disaster management.

2. Infamous case of Columbia meat packing firm:

The reach of drones in investigative journalism can be best established by the infamous case of the Columbia meat packing firm. In 2012, a camera drone hovering over the Trinity River near Dallas noticed spots of blood-red spots in the River. It turned out that pig blood was being emptied via an underground pipe from the firm located on a creek that feeds into the river. The company was indicted on 18 criminal counts and a trial is pending.

3. To investigate a leak by Edward Snowden

In July 2014, Nimrod Kamer travelled to Nassau with a drone to investigate a leak by Edward Snowden that suggested that the NSA is listening to phone calls made in the Bahamas.

4.   Harlem 2014 tragedy

The Daily Dot used a Phantom drone for first hand footage of a building that collapsed in Harlem on March 2014. This was the first live footage of manmade disaster in the world.

5.   Use of drones during Thailand and Ukraine protests

Since the use of drones for journalism, drone journalism and war journalism go side by side. We saw its glimpses during the Thailand and Ukraine protests that shook the roots of world democracy. Russia Today explored Unmanned Air Vehicles' use for several years and recently covered protests in Turkey and Ukraine to test the technology.

6. Droughts of Midwest 2012

The University of Nebraska - Lincoln's Drone Journalism Lab used drones to cover the devastating droughts that hit the Midwest in 2012.

7. Floods of the River Severn

The winter flooding in the UK provided the latest opportunity to test the capabilities of UAVs for video news gathering. A DJI Phantom 2 quadcopter filmed the floods of the River Severn in and around Worcester, capturing the scale of the floods.

8. Drone used for footage of Costa Concordia

60 minutes used a drone to get some otherwise hard-to-get footage of the half-sunken Costa Concordia, a passenger ship that ran aground in Tuscany.

9. Drone maker DJI

The applications of drones in journalism took an amazing turn when drone maker DJI demonstrated a spectacular video of its

Phantom drone flying into a volcano in the Tanna island of Vanuatu.

10 Future of drone journalism:

Now it's time for a sneak peek into the future of drone journalism. Berkeley Techraking saw some of the most fascinating ideas which if put to pieces would bring about a revolution in the world of journalism. **Andrew Donohue** proposed a technology that would allow the drones to collect air samples from high polluted areas and transmit the data to mobile app. The app would notify the users of the effected community when the pollution level of that area reaches the notified level. It would be an effort to control the pollution by transmitting data over space and time.

* * * * *

Chapter- 6

Drones Journalism:
A story telling medium

Drones will allow us to tell stories in unique and innovative ways. Drones are increasingly becoming part of the newsgathering process, allowing media organizations to capture different perspectives of events and providing them access to new locations. Filming aerials from a drone is also more immersive than from a helicopter it is part of the scene rather than just an observer above the scene.‖

The Fourth Industrial Revolution (4IR), the digital era in which we are currently living, has brought with it significant and rapid technological developments, from artificial intelligence, to machines to virtual reality. These new technologies are transforming industries, as we know them and unleashing a world of new possibilities, and drone technology is no exception.

From aiding farmers and oil and gas operators to inspecting buildings and helping emergency services, the use of drone technology is improving companies' efficiency in detecting issues, as well as with their commercial operations.

As a society living in 4IR and surrounded by an abundance of screens and devices, we are more visually literate than ever before. The omnipresence of mobile phone cameras and social media has meant that we increasingly want to consume content on our devices, and as a result, most news outlets are moving more of their content online and shrinking the size of their newsrooms. Short, timely videos have become more and more important to media organisations as a strategy for storytelling, and drones are increasingly being used as a tool for creating visual art in videography and journalism. While the use of this technology is still relatively new in reporting, it is rapidly gathering steam as more news organisations realise the value of this alternative data and footage-gathering tool.

The use of drones is allowing journalists to tell stories in ways they have never been able to before, enabling them to gather previously unobtainable footage and report in new areas, at a relatively low cost. Video footage captured by drone technology can bring the visual element of reporting to life, and can be used for standalone news features, as well as to supplement event and breaking news coverage, particularly around natural disasters or in conflict zones, areas that have previously been difficult for journalists to get access to. Unlike recent media video footage that is created using a camera attached to a helicopter or blimp, drones can get much closer to the action and can fly through forests or mountainous areas, to places that have been affected by natural disasters, and as cameras get more advanced every year, provide clear, accurate and non-intrusive footage.

Major global news outlets are increasingly recognizing the value in using drone technology as a way of providing their readers with insightful, unbiased, and up-to-date footage. The BBC has been using drone technology since 2013 and has its own in-house drone journalism team, and CNN was also an early adopter of using this technology in news reporting, and set up its own aerial unit in 2016, which has since allowed for powerful storytelling. An example of where drone technology provided invaluable insight to CNN was a trip by its crew to Kathmandu, Nepal, a couple of years after an earthquake had hit the region and rain had formed a landslide, which the crew couldn't get past. A drone was launched a few miles up the river valley and found that several other villages were devastated, and the crew took its findings to Nepalese authorities and were able to get humanitarian aid to the people who needed it.

In addition, drones are proving to be very effective when it comes to reporting on sporting events, providing high definition footage and a birds-eye aerial view; a visual that most people couldn't get through conventional means. Fox Sports, for example, now uses drones to capture footage for its millions of viewers at a range of outdoor sporting events from auto-racing, to golf, to skiing and this footage is transforming the user experience.

While the use of drones for journalism hasn't come without legal and ethical issues and some argue that drones could seriously invade people's privacy, particularly as citizen reporting using drone footage has increased, they have the potential to be used in very positive ways and to –democratise‖ aerial imagery.

No longer does it cost thousands of dollars to rent a helicopter or plane to capture images from above, and the opportunity for citizens and journalists to use drones for similar goals or even to collaborate on projects is a real possibility for the future.

While it is extremely important that journalists, and citizens, understand the laws in the country they are filming, their use should be tightly regulated. If used correctly, drones can take readers to new places and grant unexpected insights. They can enhance storytelling and enable journalists to better inform and serve the public, helping us to get smarter and gain a better perspective and understanding on global events and breaking news as it happens.

The practical use of the aforementioned lowest-budged UAVs is very limited in real-word newsgathering services, drones with costs starting at 2,000€ can operate for over an hour in quite demanding scenarios (e.g. breaking news reporting, environmental journalism, sports coverage, dissemination storytelling in tourism and broader commercial actions, focused documentaries and others) (Corcoran, 2015). Reliability is a very crucial parameter that is depended on many related factors, such as weather conditions, Wi-Fi status and reliance, remote operation range, accuracy of the data provided by the embedded sensors and other unexpected situations, thus requiring for more sophisticated design and manufacture. Furthermore, the drone flying autonomy is linked to the technology and weight of the associated batteries (or fuel tanks), as well as the involved lifting motors. Likewise, high quality capturing of photos and videos require larger, heavier and more expensive optical lenses (and overall electronics). As weight increases, the safety precautions become more important for all the operating users, the public and the drone equipment itself. Therefore, dedicated know-how is needed for controlling UAVs in real newsgathering situations, for carefully scheduling proper operation and maintenance of all the involved systems before, during and after the flight.

The motivation of the proposed model stems from the particularities residing in contemporary digital storytelling and media coverage, where multiple users and publication channels are involved in capturing and sharing events, experiences and places. It is very common for professional media organizations to utilize UGC content in their broadcasting /streaming program. Besides the streams that are captured and shared through mobile devices, drone footage from both journalists and hobbyist is usually involved. Moreover, terrestrial audiovisual surveillance modules (including UGVs –Unmanned Ground Vehicles) and integrated monitoring networks can be part of such multi-channel media coverage systems.

Given that exploitation of the various content versions may lead to significant content enhancement, difficulties regarding their detection and synchronization have to be overcome. Hence, some events can be initially identified based only on audio features, thus performing a coarse /cost-effective annotation. Refinement is possible through motion analysis and image-matching (i.e. near-duplicate detection and other similar techniques), while GPS and time-related information can be further utilized along with user-provided metadata. In general, different users will focus on the part of the story they find interesting (in any context), so practically they capture different parts and/or views of the same event (Dimoulas & Symeonidis 2016).

This plurality of streams offers the wanted multiple viewpoints, which can be combined and enhanced, augmenting audience interaction and engagement through immersive storytelling experiences (i.e. multi-view selection, AR projection, location and language adaptation, channel- and terminal-oriented playback, 3Dreproduction, panoramic and time-lapse virtual navigation, etc.). Specifically, in the newsgathering case, reporters (professional journalists and/or UGC-users) impose their own subjective point of view, either unintentionally or purposely (this is usually reflected on the involved audiovisual captures, but also on the textual comments and reportages).

Hence, a wider, more complete and versatile view of the event can be offered, purposing to meet audience demands in a more personalized manner. Apparently, advanced machine learning (i.e. deep learning) and multimodal semantic processing algorithms are required for both synchronizing and documenting all the footage of the associated Journal of Media Critiques [JMC] – Vol.3 No.11 2017 195 events, as well as for adapting the storytelling to the personalized needs of the audience (Dimoulas & Symeonidis 2016; Papadopoulos et al., 2015).

*****

Chapter – 7

10 Top Techniques to become a successful Drone Journalist

Drones are becoming increasingly widespread in journalism. This should not come as a surprise: as drone and camera tech matures, it becomes not only better but also more affordable. Modern drones can fly higher, faster, are easier to handle, and can carry high-resolution cameras. In the hands of a skilled operator, drones are capable of generating breathtaking footage that would otherwise be far beyond the realm of possibility.

1. Film something you can't film from the ground

The cardinal sin of drone journalism is flying when unnecessary. Drones are annoying; they're expensive, and risky. Why would you want to fly when you don't have to? There are plenty of other options that you should attempt to use first satellite images, Google Earth, even standing on tall buildings or on hills.
But there are legitimate reasons to use a drone, and these are the key to using the drone as a tool, and not just a gimmick. Think immediacy and access is the thing you're trying to film happening now? If an image is not available on satellite imagery, drones may be the only way to see it. Ditto for flat terrain, and anywhere with restricted ground access.

2. Know the laws

Most countries now have some version of laws regarding drone use on their books, and it's imperative to know the law before you fly. Here is a partial list of worldwide drone laws. General guidelines are: Do not fly over buildings, roads, or people; stay below 400ft altitude, and stay well away from airports, helipads, and sensitive installations. There may also be special regulations depending on what you want to do with the footage commercial operations (flying for money) are different than flying for fun. How you will be operating as a journalist is probably a gray area between the two…so be as careful and as knowledgeable as you can! Flying in wide open areas like a dam are safe, and usually legal. ©Johnny Miller / Code for Africa

3. Map where you're going to fly before you get there

Just like flying an airplane, it's important to create a flight plan before you send the drone up into the air. You don't have to use anything too fancy: Google Earth is an excellent resource to see elevation, terrain, roads and buildings. Knowing where you will take off and land from, as well as secondary landing zones in case of emergencies, is also important.
You can also use a variety of mapping data to plan what you want to look at with the drone. Depending on your location, there may be maps that show environmental data, census data, or previous survey data to help you plan your flights. You may find that it's easier (and cheaper) to just use satellite imagery that's already been created!

4. Long, steady shots work better

The easiest way to tell if someone is an experienced drone pilot is by looking at the length of the steady shots they take in their video. Aerial videography is exciting, interesting, and can contain a lot of visual information. You want to give your viewers the longest possible time to absorb that information before making a cut, or adjusting the direction of the drone. So when you hold a shot, don't touch the yaw! The yaw turns the drone from side to side, and will immediately ruin a long tracking shot. If you find yourself drifting slightly off course, continue to hold the shot as-is, and then come back and repeat it. You might find the original, ‒off-center‖ shot works better!

Generally you are looking at reveals, pushes, tracking, and point-of-interest style shots. These four types of shots will be you're bread-and-butter, and it's important that you practice them again and again in a controlled environment, before you take the drone out into the field.

5. Your footage won't stand alone

Drones are an incredible tool for a journalist, but they rarely can tell the whole story. You will inevitably be creating additional resources to build a great story, including written work, stills and video from the ground, and data visualizations. Don't oversell your ability to tell a story only from the air. Package the drone concept to your editor as a valuable tool that can give your viewers a new perspective, but one that works best as an adjunct to your original skill set. Tools like Shorthand can create amazing, immersive storytelling like this.

6. Know when to say no.

Drones are dangerous, and can be ethically ambiguous. There is not a good set of precedents for how drones and drone footage can be legally used, which means operating them sometimes falls into a gray area. Use your intuition. Think of how you would react if you were witnessing someone else flying the drone in the same way. And crucially, don't be bullied by someone who is overselling the drone as a gimmick, or wanting you to use it in unsafe conditions. Remember to only use the drone as a last resort using satellite images or taking photos from the ground is a much safer option. And finally, know that legally, the operator (You!) is the one responsible for anything that goes wrong not your editor.

Borowick recited FAA guidelines for safe and legal operation of drones. Among them:

1. Do not fly higher than 400 feet or within five miles of any airport, public or private.
2. Keep your drone in eyesight at all times; use an observer if assistance is needed
3. Do not fly in adverse weather conditions, such as high winds or reduced visibility
4. Do not fly after dark unless you have permission

Top 3 challenges of drones in journalism:

1. Drone journalism will always be challenged by government regulations, public opinion and the foolish actions of a minority. As far as government regulations go, we can only be vigilant and hope these overseers will be reasonable and not stifle an industry with cumbersome and unnecessary regulations.
2. The media needs to band together and lobby for a workable regulatory regime. But the media by its very nature doesn't tend to work towards a common goal preferring exclusivity above all else. If we are to move this forward, the media must change the way it does things and work together for the benefit of an industry.
3. Public opinion is the technology's greatest challenge. Regardless of regulations or assurances, the public remains paranoid about what the technology will be used for. Many see it as an invasion of privacy and think drone journalists will be flying through their communities looking for stories, and ready to swoop down from on high when they are found.
4. Nothing could be further from the truth. Further complicating this is that the public cannot, or are unwilling to, differentiate between professional operators and recreational, or even worse, out-of-the-box users.

Opportunities for drones in journalism:
1. Greater depth and perspective in storytelling
2. Timely coverage of events
3. Cost effective coverage of events

Top 3 opportunities for drones in journalism:
1. Drone Data
I think there's some interesting potential around sensor and image data that could offer another key element to the practice of drone journalism. Equipping UAVs with environmental, pollution or other sensors, with the aim of gathering data sets for either news verification or to reveal new stories, could be a rich opportunity in years to come. Equally, bolting image recognition and crowd counting software onto UAVs could provide data through which

_official figures' can be scrutinized. Drone data journalism could be an exciting area in the coming years. Drones used within engineering or humanitarian scenarios are beginning to explore this space, and journalism could follow suit.

2. Unique affordances of aerial footage

This is such an obvious one but is worth remembering. Aerial footage from natural disasters, conflict zones, public demonstrations or mass sporting events can be a genuinely powerful and unique way to convey a story. It creates a unique dynamic for storytellers. Literally providing a different perspective. Journalists should remember the power of such footage, and deploy it to maximum editorial advantage rather than let it become _run of the mill'.

3. Dissemination to local newsrooms

Although there is a focus on high-end story treatments, i.e. VR and 360 footage.

Mega Opportunities for drones in journalism:

The main opportunities for drones in journalism endeavors can be defined as follows:

1. Technical improvements

As companies keep producing new models of drones, these new versions possess enhanced features as the hold position or the possibility of navigating through trees and other obstacles due to an advanced sensing system.

2. Pricing/Popularity

As with any technology, the affordability is a key aspect to ensure the popularity of any device; while prices of advanced drones are dropping, more newsrooms -regardless of size or scope can acquire and start to play with them.

3.   Diversity of usage

In journalism, a reporter is asked to be versatile; that could also be applied to his/her tools for the coverage. Drones are being used to report breaking news, to produce documentaries or to cover sports events.

*****

Conclusion

Drones offer interesting perspectives for media and journalism industry. Drones equipped with cameras can take photos and videos from an aerial perspective, reaching inaccessible places or offering breathtaking footage. Still, journalists might hesitate to use drones for their work, because there are too many issues and unclear regulations. In the long-term, it is expected that drones will add another newsgathering tool for journalists that would be combined with all the other contemporary media technologies (Corcoran 2015; Chapa 2013; Jarvis 2014; Mancosu 2016).

The main points are:

1. For geographic and war reporting, drones offer unprecedented access in combination with safety for a journalist's body.
2. Drones are relatively inexpensive gadgets inviting experimentation, but expert use requires training and experience.
3. Citizens and policymakers remain skeptical towards drone use. Privacy violations, conflicts with authorities, or damages need to be kept in a drone journalist's mind.
4. The decision to invest in drone journalism should be guided by your editorial policy and the news themes your newsroom is prioritizing.

Next, the positive and negative outcomes of drone journalism. There is clearly a potential in the use of drones to cover situations that are dangerous or inaccessible for journalists, at a relatively low cost. On the other hand, there is no control on that access (e.g. no press card for drones) and a general drone use can foster surveillance culture. The drone journalism will be a niche in the evolving news environment and outline different scenarios for different newsrooms, showing how:

1. large media might choose to engage for cost-cutting reasons,
2. average media should only invest when aligned with their editorial policy,
3. Freelancers could develop a successful specialty in drone journalism.

A birds' eye on Drone Journalism

Drones are also known as ‒unmanned aerial systems (UAS)‖ or ‒remotely piloted aircraft systems (RPAS)‖. Drones equipped with cameras can take photos and videos from an aerial perspective that can be integrated into everyday news coverage. Reporters can either directly integrate the material into their online or TV news outlets, or they can indirectly make use of the materials as a source to feed their stories (especially in ethically critical cases).

It's a bird… It's a plane… It's a drone
There exist several types of drones, each with different advantages and difficulties:
All journalists and media professionals should keep in mind the skepticism of the population and lawmakers towards drone use. Especially regarding their audiences, journalists have to consider carefully if the new way of reporting and overcoming barriers equals a possible loss of journalistic credibility caused by privacy violations, conflicts with authorities, or damages. However, you can benefit from a bird's view on the world which allows increased access, potential new revenues and markets, unprecedented geographic and war reporting and safety for a journalist's body. Another key point is that, in exchange for all the advantages they provide, drones are relatively inexpensive gadgets.

For media organizations, it is a rather strategic decision whether to invest in drone journalism or not. Large media corporations that already use a news helicopter should definitely take a look on the resources they can save if they invest in drones. Important in that case is to take into account the amount of training their journalists need before being professional drone journalists.

Average or small media companies should only invest in drone journalism if it benefits their journalist working on investigative, war, sports, and geographic reporting. If your team rarely works in these fields, it might be better not to invest in drone journalism, unless, they want to broaden their coverage into these fields.

Freelancers who decide to go for drone journalism could succeed as a highly specialized media worker with their own enterprise in an emerging business. But in a precarious working environment, they should consider being exploited by major media. As a consequence, their situation could worsen, since self-employed journalists carry the financial risks of the purchase and training alone.

As described above, drone journalism will be a niche in the evolving news environment. Drone recorded materials will probably be bought and sold a lot since economically, it is more cost-efficient for small and average media companies. Probably, they will rather buy professional drone shots and videos than invest in their own drone journalist. As a start-up or as a big player the in media business, however, investing in drone journalism to fill this niche might be fruitful. After all, when it comes to drone journalism, the sky is the limit.

–If there is a distinctive path that modern technological change has followed, it is that technology goes where it has never been,‖ Langdon Winner, a political scientist, wrote in 1980. The development of drones, surely enough, has followed this progression. As this book chronicles, within a few short years of coalescing as technological artifacts, drones have been deployed to the corners of the world, from the Arctic to the Antarctic, in mountains and in desert valleys below sea level, in cities and above isolated villages.

It is a truism that drone technology is rapidly changing. But this is not the whole truth. Some aspects are changing rapidly; others, such as propellers, are changing slowly, if at all. As a rule, those parts of a drone that have to do with information collection and processing are likely to continue to develop at a brisk pace; the parts that have to do with the physical movement of a drone through the air are also changing, but not as dramatically. Crucial infection points in the development of drones have come when innovations in microelectronics have enabled innovations in physical movement. This is true of the accelerometer and gyroscope data that make it possible for quadcopter to maintain stability, and of GPS devices that allow drones to navigate from one point in space to another.

References

Chamberlain, Phillip. (2017): Drones and Journalism. New York In: Routledge.

Chapa, Lilly. (2013): _Drone journalism begins slow take off‘ In: News media and the law 2013 37(2): 9-10.

Cooke, Nancy., Rowe, Leah. & Winston, Bennett., (2017): Remotely piloted aircraft systems: a human systems integration perspective In: Chichester, West Sussex, United Kingdom John Wiley & Sons, Inc.

Corcoran, Mark., (2012): _Drone journalism takes off‘, ABC News. In: http://www.abc.net.au/news/2012-02-21/drone-journalism-takes-off/3840616 [Accessed Oct 10, 2016].

Corcoran, Mark., (2015): _Drone Journalism: Newsgathering applications of Unmanned Aerial Vehicles (UAVs) in covering conflict, civil unrest and disaster‘ In: https://assets.documentcloud.org/documents/1034066/final-drone-journalism-duringconflict-civil.pdf [Accessed Oct. 10, 2016].

Culver, Kathleen Bartzen (2014): _From battlefield to newsroom: Ethical implications of drone technology in journalism‘ In: Journal of Mass Media Ethics, 2014 29:52–64.

Dimoulas, Charalampos., Veglis, Andreas., & Kalliris, George. (2014): –Application of Mobile Cloud-Based Technologies in News Reporting: Current Trends and Future Perspectives‖. In: J. Rodrigues, K. Lin, & J. Lloret (Eds.), Mobile Networks and Cloud Computing Convergence for Progressive Services and Applications, IGI, pp. 320-343.

Dimoulas, Charalampos, & Symeonidis, Andreas (2015): _Syncing shared multimedia through audiovisual bimodal segmentation' In: Papadopoulos S., Cesar P., Shamma D.A. & Kelliher S. (Eds.) Special issue on Social Multimedia and Storytelling. MultiMedia IEEE 2015 22(3): 26-42.

Dorroh, Jennifer. (2015): _Environmental Reporting and Media Development: Equipping Journalists with the Training and Tools to Cover a Critical Beat', Center for International Media Assistance (CIMCA) In: http://www.cima.ned.org/publication/environmental-reporting-media-development/ [Accessed Feb. 1, 2017].

Goldberg, David., Corcoran, Mark., & Picard, Robert. (2013): _Remotely Piloted Aircraft Systems & Journalism', Reuters Institute for the Study of Journalism In: https://reutersinstitute.politics.ox.ac.uk/sites/default/files/R emotely%20Piloted%20Air craft%20and%20Journalism_0.pdf [Accessed Feb. 1, 2017].

Journal of Media Critiques [JMC] – Vol.3 No.11 2017 199 Gynnild, Astrid. (2014): _The Robot Eye Witness: Extending visual journalism through drone surveillance' In: Digital journalism, 2014 2(3): 334-343.

Jarvis, John. (2014): –The ethical debate of drone journalism: flying into the future of reporting‖ In:: http://opensiuc.lib.siu.edu/gs_rp/475 [Accessed Oct. 10, 2016]. Holton, Avery., Lawson, Sean., & Love, Cynthia. (2015): _Unmanned Aerial Vehicles: Opportunities, barriers, and the future of ' In: Journalism Practice 2015 9(5): 634-650.

Mancosu, Marco., (2016): Opportunities & Challenges In Drone Journalism: 15 Experts Share Their Views. Skytango In: https://skytango.com/drone-journalismopportunities-and-challenges-15-experts-share-their-views/ [Accessed February 20, 2017].

Ogleby, George. & Joshi, Cameron., (2016): Five ways drones are being used to help the environment. Edie.net In: https://www.edie.net/news/8/Drone-technologyenvironmental-sustainability-impact-for-the-UK/ [Accessed February 20, 2017].

Papadopoulos Symeon., Cesar Pablo., Shamma David & Kelliher Aisling (Eds.) (2015): _Special issue on Social Multimedia and Storytelling' In: MultiMedia IEEE 2015 22(3): 10-65.

Tremayne, Mark., & Clark, Andrew. (2014): _New perspectives from the sky: Unmanned aerial vehicles and journalism' In: Digital journalism 2014 2(2): 232-246. Waite, Matt. & Kreimer,

Whitaker, Nicholas., (2016): An interview with Matt Waite about the future of Drone Journalism, Medium In: https://medium.com/google-news-lab/drone-journalism-aninterview-with-matt-waite-about-the-future-of-drones-in-journalism7b1811c661aa#.ua2mkwlzw [Accessed Oct. 10, 2016].

Additional References

Bal, H. M., & Baruh, L. (2015). Citizen Involvement In Emergency Reporting: A Study On Witnessing And Citizen Journalism. *Interactions*: *Studies in Communication & Culture, 6*(2), 213–231.

Cohen, N. S. (2015). Entrepreneurial Journalism and the Precarious State of Media Work. *South Atlantic Quarterly, 114*(3), 513–533.

Cook, C., & Sirkkunen, E. (2013). What's in a Niche? Exploring The Business Model of Online Journalism. *Journal of Media Business Studies, 10*(4), 63–82.

Moore, J. A. (2014). Robot vs. Human. *Columbia Journalism Review, 53*(2), 6.

Picard, R. G. (2014). Twilight or New Dawn of Journalism? *Digital Journalism, 2*(3), 273–283.

Online References

https://www.researchgate.net/publication/319707325_Drone_Journalism_Generating_Immersive_Experiences

http://mediacritiques.net/index.php/jmc/article/viewFile/166/126

https://www.journalism.co.uk/tip-of-the-day/tip-become-a-master-of-drone-journalism/s419/a737419/

https://www.floridatoday.com/story/news/2018/08/23/drone-journalism/1072245002/

https://ijnet.org/en/story/five-things-you-need-know-about-drone-journalism

https://medium.com/journalism-trends-technologies/keeping-an-eagle-eye-on-drone-journalism-cc907afbde30

https://whatis.techtarget.com/definition/drone-journalism

https://en.wikipedia.org/wiki/Drone_journalism

https://books.google.co.in/books?id=xNJMDwAAQBAJ&printsec=frontcover&dq=drone+journalism&hl=en&sa=X&ved=0ahUKEwjzyv2QnLTiAhXCbX0KHVbNCjYQ6AEIKjAA#v=onepage&q=drone%20journalism&f=false

https://books.google.co.in/books?id=1M0NDgAAQBAJ&printsec=frontcover&dq=drone+journalism&hl=en&sa=X&ved=0ahUKEwjzyv2QnLTiAhXCbX0KHVbNCjYQ6AEILzAB#v=onepage&q=drone%20journalism&f=false
https://dronecenter.bard.edu/drones-in-india/

https://www.drdo.gov.in/drdo/pub/npc/2017/february/din-27Feb2017.pdf

https://www.firstpost.com/tech/news-analysis/india-gets-its-first-drone-policy-all-you-need-to-know-about-drone-regulations-1-0-5060601.html

https://medium.com/frontier-technology-livestreaming/drone-regulations-in-india-simplified-f5740d088670

https://www.orfonline.org/wp-content/uploads/2018/03/ORF_OccasionalPaper_145_Drones.pdf

https://www.dronitech.com/how-drones-are-transforming-the-media-industry/

https://www.cbinsights.com/research/drone-impact-society-uav/

http://www.nishithdesai.com/fileadmin/user_upload/pdfs/Research%20Papers/Unravelling_The_Future_Game_of_Drones.pdf

https://gmisummit.com/wp-content/uploads/2018/10/Drone-Journalism-Article-15-May-2018-2.pdf

https://www.millefoto.com/blog/2017/1/26/5n1igknvf52dctuet3hpkc1t6xouw8

Index